Dion Boucicault

The Streets of New York

Dion Boucicault

The Streets of New York

ISBN/EAN: 9783337335069

Printed in Europe, USA, Canada, Australia, Japan

Cover: Foto ©Andreas Hilbeck / pixelio.de

More available books at **www.hansebooks.com**

A DRAMA IN FIVE ACTS

BY

DION BOUCICAULT

―――――

CHICAGO
THE DRAMATIC PUBLISHING COMPANY

THE STREETS OF NEW YORK.

CAST OF CHARACTERS.

Wallack's Theatre, December, 1857

CAPTAIN FAIRWEATHER,......................Mr. Blake.

GIDEON BLOODGOOD,................. ....Mr. Norton.

BADGER,......................................Mr. Lester.

MARK LIVINGSTONE,......................Mr. Sothern.

PAUL,..Mr. A. H. Davenport

PUFFY,......................................Mr. Sloan.

DAN......................................Mr. T. B. Johnson.

DANIELS,......................................Mr. Tree.

EDWARDS,......................................Mr. Levere.

MRS. FAIRWEATHER,......................Mrs. Blake.

MRS. PUFFY,...................... .. Mrs. Cooke.

ALIDA,... ....Mrs. Hoey.

LUCY,........................ ....Mrs. J. H. Allen.

COSTUMES—Modern.

The first act occurs during the commercial panic of 1837. The remainder of the drama takes place during the panic of 1857.

STAGE DIRECTIONS.

L. means *First Entrance, Left.* R. *First Entrance, Right.* S. E. L. *Second Entrance, Left.* S. E. R. *Second Entrance, Right.* U. E. L. *Upper Entrance, Left.* U. E. R. *Upper Entrance, Right.* C. *Centre.* L. C. *Left Centre.* R. C. *Right of Centre.* T. E. L. *Third Entrance, Left.* T. E. R. *Third Entrance, Right.* C. D. *Centre Door.* D. R. *Door Right.* D. L. *Door Left.* U. D. L. *Upper Door, Left.* U. D. R. *Upper Door, Right.* D. F. *Door in flat.*

*** The reader is supposed to be on the stage, facing the audience.

THE STREETS OF NEW YORK.

ACT I.

THE PANIC OF 1837.

SCENE.—*The private office of a banking house in New York; door at back, leading to the bank; door* L. H., *leading to a side street.* **Gideon Bloodgood** *seated,* C., *at desk.*

[*Enter* **Edwards**, L. H. D. F., *with a sheet of paper.*]

Edw. The stock list, sir ;—second board of brokers.

Blood. [*Rising eagerly.*] Let me see it. Tell the cashier to close the bank on the stroke of three, and dismiss the clerks. [*Reads. Exit* **Edwards.**] So—as I expected, every stock is down further still, and my last effort to retrieve my fortune has plunged me into utter ruin? [*Crushes up the paper.*] To-morrow, my drafts to the amount of eighty thousand dollars will be protested. To-morrow, yonder street, now so still, will be filled with a howling multitude, for the house of Bloodgood, the banker, will fail, and in its fall will crush hundreds, thousands, who have their fortunes laid up here.

[*Re-enter* **Edwards.**]

Edw. Here are the keys of the safe, sir, and the vault. [*Leaves keys on desk and shows a check to* **Bloodgood.**] The building committee of St. Peter's new church have applied for your donation. It is a thousand dollars.

Blood. Pay it. [*Exit* **Edwards.**] To-morrow, New York will ring from Union Square to the Battery with the news— " Bloodgood has absconded "—but to-morrow I shall be safe on board the packet for Liverpool—all is prepared for my flight with my only care in life, my only hope—my darling child— her fortune secure—— [*Rises.*] The affair will blow over;

3

Bloodgood's bankruptcy will soon be forgotten in the whirl of New York trade, but Alida, my dear Alida, will be safe from want.

[*Re-enter* **Edwards.**]

Edw. Here, sir, are the drafts on the Bank of England, $70,000. [*Hands papers to* **Bloodgood,** *who places them in his pocket-book.*]

Blood. Are the clerks all gone?

Edw. All, sir, except Mr. Badger.

Blood. Badger! the most negligent of all! That is strange.

Edw. His entries are behindhand, he says, and he is balancing his books.

Blood. Desire him to come to me. [*Sits. Exit* **Edwards.**]

[*Enter* **Badger,** *smoking cigar.*]

Bad. You have asked for me?

Blood. Yes; you are strangely attentive to business to-day, Mr. Badger.

Bad. Everything has a beginning.

Blood. Then you will please to begin to-morrow.

Bad. To-morrow! no sir, my business must be done to-day. *Carpe diem*—make most of to-day—that's my philosophy.

Blood. Mr. Badger, philosophy is not a virtue in a banker's clerk.

Bad. Think not?

Blood. [*Impatiently.*] Neither philosophy nor impertinence. You are discharged from my employment.

Bad. Pardon me! I do not catch the precise word.

Blood. [*Sternly.*] Go, sir, go! I discharge you.

Bad. Go!—discharge me? I am still more in the dark. I can understand my services not being required in a house that goes on, but where the house is ready to burst up the formality of telling a clerk he is discharged does seem to me an unnecessary luxury.

Blood. [*Troubled.*] I do not understand you, sir.

Bad. [*Seating himself on a desk, deliberately dangling his legs.*] No! well I'll dot my i's and cross my t's, and make myself plain to the meanest capacity. In business there are two ways of getting rich, one hard, slow and troublous: this is called labor

Blood. Sir!

Bad. Allow me to finish. The other easy, quick and

demanding nothing but a pliant conscience and a daring mind —is now pleasantly denominated financiering—but when New York was honest, it was called fraudulent bankruptcy, that was before you and I were born.

Blood. What do you mean ?

Bad. I mean that for more than two years I have watched your business transactions ; when you thought me idle, my eyes were everywhere : in your books, in your safe, in your vaults ; if you doubt me question me about your operations for the last three months.

Blood. This is infamous !

Bad. That is precisely the word I used when I came to the end of your books.

Edw. [*Outside.*] This way, sir.

[*Enter* **Edwards**, *with* **Captain Fairweather.**]

Blood. [*To* **Badger**, *in alarm.*] Not a word.

Bad. All right.

Edw. [*Introducing* **Captain Fairweather.**] This is Mr. Bloodgood.

Capt. Glad to see you, sir. You will pardon my intruding at an hour when the bank, I am told, is closed.

Blood. I am at your service, sir. [*He makes a sign for* **Badger** *to retire, but the latter remains.*]

Bad. [*To* **Captain.**] You may speak, sir ; Mr. Bloodgood has no secrets from me. I am in his confidence.

Capt. [*Sits.*] I am a sea captain, in the India trade. My voyages are of the longest, and thus I am obliged to leave my wife and two children almost at the mercy of circumstances. I was spending a happy month with my darlings at a little cozy place I have at Yonkers while my ship was loading, when this infernal commercial squall set in—all my fortune, $100,000, the fruits of thirty years' hard toil—was invested in the United States Bank—it was the livelihood of my wife—the food of my little children—I hurried to my brokers and sold out. I saved myself just in time.

Blood. I admire your promptitude.

Capt. To-morrow I sail for China ; for the last three weeks I have worried my brains to think how I should bestow my money—to-day I bethought me of your house—the oldest in New York—your name stands beyond suspicion, and if I leave this money in your hands, I can sleep nightly with the happy assurance that whatever happens to me, my dearest ones are safe.

Bad. You may pull your nightcap over your ears with that established conviction.

Capt. Now, I know your bank is closed, but if you will accept this money as a special deposit, I will write to you how I desire it to be invested hereafter.

Blood. [*Pensive.*] You have a family?

Capt. Don't talk of them—tears of joy come into my eyes whenever I think of those children—and my dear wife, the patient, devoted companion of the old sailor, whose loving voice murmurs each evening a prayer for those who are on the sea ; and my children, sir, two little angels ; one a fair little thing —we call her Lucy—she is the youngest—all red and white like a little bundle of flowers ; and my eldest—my son Paul—we named him after Paul Jones—a sailor's whim ; well, sir, when the ship is creaking and groaning under my feet, when the squall drives the hail and sleet across my face, amidst the thunder, I only hear three voices—through the gloom I can see only three faces, pressed together like three angels waiting for me in heaven, and that heaven is my home. But, how I do talk, sir—forgetting that these things can't interest you.

Blood. They do, more than you imagine. I, too, have a child—only one—a motherless child !

Capt. Ain't it good to speak of the little beings ? Don't it fill the heart like a draught of sweet water ? My darling torments, here is their fortune—I have it in my hand—it is here— I have snatched it from the waves ; I have won it across the tempest ; I have labored, wrestled, and suffered for it ; but it seemed nothing, for it was for them. Take it, sir. [*He hands a pocket-book.*] In this pocket-book you will find one hundred thousand dollars. May I take your receipt, and at once depart for my vessel ?

Bad. [*Aside.*] This is getting positively interesting.

Blood. Your confidence flatters me, sir. You desire to place this money with me as a special deposit ?

Capt. If you please. Will you see that the amount is correct ?

Blood. [*Counting.*] Mr. Badger, prepare the receipt.

Bad. [*Writing.*] " New York, 13th of December, 1837. Received, on special deposit, from——" [*To* **Captain.**] Your name, sir ?

Capt. Captain Fairweather, of the ship Paul and Lucy, of New York.

Bad. [*Writing.*] Captain Fairweather, of the ship——

Blood. One hundred thousand dollars—quite correct.

Bad. [*Handing receipt to* **Bloodgood,** *and watching him closely as he takes the pen.*] Please sign the receipt. [*Aside.*] His hand does not tremble, not a muscle moves. What a magnificent robber !

Blood. [*To* **Captain.**] Here is your receipt.

Capt. A thousand thanks. Now I am relieved of all trouble.

Bad. [*Aside.*] That's true.

Capt. I must return in haste to the Astor House, where I dine with my owners at four—I fear I am late. Good-day, Mr. Bloodgood.

Blood. Good-day, Captain, and a prosperous voyage to you. [*Exit* **Captain Fairweather. Badger** *opens ledger.*] What are you doing, Mr. Badger.

Bad. I am going to enter that special deposit in the ledger.

Blood. Mr. Badger !

Bad. Mr. Bloodgood ?

Blood. [*Brings him down.*] I have been deceived in you. I confess I did not know your value.

Bad. [*Modestly.*] Patience and perseverance, sir, tells in the long run.

Blood. Here are one thousand dollars—I present them to you for your past services.

Bad. [*Takes the money, and walks over to the ledger on the desk, which he closes significantly.*] And for the present service ?

Blood. What do you mean ?

Bad. My meaning is as clear as Croton. I thought you were going to fail—I see I was wrong—you are going to abscond.

Blood. Mr. Badger ! this language——

Bad. This deposit is special ; you dare not use it in your business ; your creditors cannot touch it—ergo, you mean to make a raise and there's but one way—absconsion ! absquatulation.

Blood. [*Smiling.*] It is possible that this evening I may take a little walk out of town.

Bad. In a steamboat ?

Blood. Meet me at Peck Slip, at five o'clock, and I will hand you double the sum I gave you.

Bad. [*Aside.*] In all three thousand dollars.

[*Re-enter* **Edwards.**]

Edw. Your daughter, sir ; Miss Alida is in the carriage at the door and is screaming to be admitted.

Blood. Tell the nurse to pacify her for a few moments.

Edw. She dare not, sir; Miss Alida has torn nurse's face in a fearful manner already. [*Exit.*]

Bad. Dear, high-spirited child! If she is so gentle now, what will she be when she is twenty, and her nails are fully developed!

Blood. [*Takes hat.*] I will return immediately. [*Exit.*]

Bad. [*Following* **Bloodgood** *with his eyes.*] Oh, nature, wonderful mistress! Keep close to your daughter, Bloodgood, for she is your master! Ruin, pillage, rob fifty families to make her rich with their misery, happy in their tears. I watched him as he received the fortune of that noble old sailor—not a blink— his heart of iron never quailed; but in this heart of iron there is a straw, a weakness by which it may be cracked, and that weakness is his own child—children! They are the devil in disguise. I have not got any except my passions, my vices—a large family of spoilt and ungrateful little devils, who threaten their loving father with a prison.

Edw. [*Outside.*] I tell you, sir, he is not in.

Capt. [*Outside.*] Let me pass, I say. [*He enters very much agitated.*] Where is he? Where is he?

Bad. [*Surprised.*] What is the matter, sir?

Capt. Mr. Bloodgood—I must see him—speak to him this instant, do you not hear me?

Bad. But——

Capt. He has not gone.

Bad. Sir——

Capt. Ah, he is here!

[Re-enter Bloodgood.]

Blood. What is the meaning of this?

Capt. Ah! you—it is you—[*Trying to restrain his emotion.*] Sir, I have changed my mind; here is your receipt; have the goodness to return me the deposit I—I—left with you.

Blood. Sir!

Capt. I have another investment for this sum, and I—beg you to restore it to me.

Blood. Restore it! you have a very strange way, sir, of demanding what is due to you.

Capt. It is true; pardon me, but I have told you it is all I possess. It is the fortune of my wife, of my children, of my brave Paul, and my dear little Lucy. It is their future happiness, their life! Listen, sir; I will be frank with you. Just now, on returning to my hotel, I found the owners of my ship waiting dinner for me, well, they were speaking as merchants will speak of each other—your name was mentioned—I listened—and they said—it makes me tremble even now—they said there were rumors abroad to-day that your house was in peril.

Blood. I attach no importance, sir, to idle talk.

Capt. But I attach importance to it, sir. How can I leave the city with this suspicion on my mind that perhaps I have compromised the future of my family.

Blood. Sir !

Capt. Take back your receipt, and return me my money.

Blood. You know, sir, that it is after banking hours. Return to-morrow.

Capt. No. You received my deposit after banking hours.

Blood. I am not a paying teller, to count out money.

Capt. You did not say so when you counted it in.

[*Enter* **Edwards.**]

Edw. The driver says you will be late for the——

Blood. [*Trying to stop him.*] That will do. [*Exit* **Edwards.**]

Capt. What did he say? [*Runs to the window.*] A carriage at the door——

Bad. [*Aside.*] Things are getting complicated here.

Capt. Yes—I see it all. He is going to fly with the fortunes and savings of his dupes ! [*Tearing his cravat.*] Ah ! I shall choke ! [*Furiously to* **Bloodgood.**] But I am here, villain, I am here in time !

Blood. Sir !

Capt. To-morrow, you said—return to-morrow—but to-morrow you will be gone. [*Precipitates himself on* **Bloodgood.**] My money, my money ! I will have it this instant ! Do not speak a word, it is useless, I will not listen to you. My money, or I will kill you as a coward should be killed. Robber ! Thief !

Bad. [*Aside.*] Hi ! hi ! This is worth fifty cents—reserved seats extra.

Blood. [*Disengaging himself.*] Enough of this scandal. You shall have your money back again.

Capt. Give it me—ah !—[*In pain.*] My head ! [*To* **Bloodgood.**] Be quick, give it to me, and let me go. [*Staggering and putting his hands to his face.*] My God ! what is this strange feeling which overcomes me.

Bad. He is falling, what's the matter of him ? [**Captain F.** *falls in chair,* C.]

Blood. His face is purple. [*Takes pocket-book and commences to count out money. Soft music to end of act.*]

Capt. I am suffocating; some air. I cannot see; everything is black before my eyes. Am I dying? Oh, no, no! it cannot be, I will not die. I must see them again. Some water—quick! Come to me—my wife—my children! Where are they that I cannot fold them in my arms! [*He looks strangely, and fearfully into the face of* **Bloodgood** *for an instant, and then breaks into a loud sob.*] Oh, my children— my poor, poor, little children! [*After some convulsive efforts to speak his eyes become fixed.*]

Blood. [*Distracted.*] Some one run for help. Badger, a doctor, quick.

Bad. [*Standing over* **Captain.**] All right, sir, I have studied medicine—that is how I learned most of my loose habits. [*Examines the* **Captain's** *pulse and eyes.*] It is useless, sir. He is dead.

Blood. [*Horrified.*] Dead! [**Bloodgood's** *attitude is one of extreme horror. This position gradually relaxes as he begins to see the advantages that will result from the* **Captain's** *death.*] Can it be possible?

Bad. [*Tearing open the* **Captain's** *vest. The receipt falls on the ground.*] His heart has ceased to beat—congestion in all its diagnostics.

Blood. Dead!

Bad. Apoplexy—the symptoms well developed—the causes natural, over-excitement and sudden emotion.

Blood. [*Relaxing into an attitude of cunning.*] Dead!

Bad. You are spared the agony of counting out his money.

Blood. Dead!

Bad. [*Sees receipt on ground.*] Ha! here is the receipt! Signed by Bloodgood. As a general rule never destroy a receipt—there is no knowing when it may yet prove useful. [*Picks it up, and puts it in his pocket.*]

[*Tableau.*]

END OF ACT I.

(A lapse of twenty years is supposed to intervene between the first and second acts.)

ACT II.

THE PANIC OF 1857.

SCENE I.—*The Park, near Tammany Hall.*

[*Enter* **Livingstone.**]

Liv. Eight o'clock in the morning. For the last hour I have been hovering round Chatham Street—I wanted to sell my overcoat to some enterprising Israelite, but I could not muster the courage to enter one of those dens. Can I realize the fact? Three months ago, I stood there, the fashionable Mark Livingstone, owner of the Waterwitch yacht, one of the original stockholders in the Academy of Music, and now, burst up, sold out, and reduced to breakfast off this coat. [*Feels in the pocket.*] What do I feel? a gold dollar—undiscovered in the Raglan of other days! [*Withdraws his hand.*] No; 'tis a five-cent piece!

[*Enter* **Puffy** *with a hot-potato arrangement.*]

Puffy. Past eight o'clock! I am late this morning.

Liv. I wonder what that fellow has in his tin volcano—it smells well. Ha! what are those funny things? Ah!

Puffy. Sweet potatoes, sir.

Liv. Indeed. [*Aside.*] If the Union Club saw me—[*Looks round.*] No: I am incog—hunger cries aloud. Here goes.

Puffy. Why, bless me, if it ain't Mr. Livingstone!

Liv. The devil! He knows me—I dare not eat a morsel.

Puffy. I'm Puffy, sir; the baker that was—in Broadway—served you, sir, and your good father afore you.

Liv. Oh, Puffy—ah, true. [*Aside.*] I wonder if I owe him anything.

Puffy. Down in the world now, sir—over-speculated like the rest on 'em. I expanded on a new-fangled oven, that was to bake enough bread in six hours to supply the whole United States—got done brown in it myself—subsided into Bowery—expanded again on waffles, caught, a second time—obliged to contract into a twelve-foot front on Division Street. Mrs. P. tends the indoor trade—I do a locomotive business in potatoes, and we let our second floor. My son Dan sleeps with George Washington No. 4, while Mrs. P. and I make out under the counter; Mrs. P., bein' wide, objects some, but I says—says I

" My dear, everybody must contract themselves in these here hard times."

Liv. So you are poor now, are you? [*Takes a potato, playfully.*]

Puffy. Yes, sir ; I ain't ashamed to own it—for I hurt nobody but myself. Take a little salt, sir. But, Lord bless you, sir, poverty don't come amiss to me—I've got no pride to support. Now, there's my lodgers——

Liv. Ah, your second floor.

Puffy. A widow lady and her two grown children—poor as mine, but proud, sir—they was grand folks once ; you can see that by the way they try to hide it. Mrs. Fairweather is a——

Liv. Fairweather—the widow of a sea captain, who died here in New York, twenty years ago ?

Puffy. Do you know my lodgers ?

Liv. Three months ago they lived in Brooklyn—Paul had clerkship in the Navy Yard.

Puffy. But when the panic set in, the United States government contracted—it paid off a number of employees, and Mr. Paul was discharged.

Liv. They are reduced to poverty and I did not know it. No, how could I. [*Aside.*] Since my ruin I have avoided them. [*Aloud.*] And Lucy—I mean Miss Fairweather ?——

Puffy. She works at a milliner's in Broadway—bless her sweet face and kind smile—me and my wife, we could bake ourselves into bread afore she and they should come to want ; and as for my boy Dan—talk of going through fire and water for her—he does that every night for nothing. Why, sir, you can't say " Lucy," but a big tear will come up in his eye as big as a cartwheel, and then he'll let out an almighty cuss, that sounds like a thousand o' brick.

[*Enter* **Paul** *and* **Mrs. Fairweather,** *dressed in black.*]

Liv. Oh ! [*In confusion hides the potato in his pocket, and hums an air as he walks away. Aside.*] I wonder if they know me.

Mrs. F. Ah, Mr. Puffy.

Puffy. What, my second floor ! Mrs. Fairweather—good-morning, Mr. Paul ; I hope no misfortune has happened—you are dressed in mourning.

Mrs. F. This is the anniversary of my poor husband's death ; this day, twenty years ago, he was taken away from us—we keep it sacred to his memory.

Paul. It was a fatal day for us. When my father left home he had $100,000 on his person—when he was found lying dead on the sidewalk of Liberty Street, he was robbed of all.

Mrs. F. From that hour misfortune has tracked us—we have lost our friends.

Puffy. Friends—that reminds me—why, where is Mr. Livingstone—there's his coat——

Paul. Livingstone !

Puffy. We were talking of you, when you came up. He slipped away.

[*Re-enter* **Livingstone.**]

Liv. I think I dropped my coat. [*Recognizing them.*] Paul—am I mistaken ?

Mrs. F. No, Mr. Livingstone.

Paul. Good-morning, sir.

Liv. Sir !—Mr. Livingstone !—have I offended you ?

Paul. We could not expect you to descend to visit us in our poor lodging.

Mrs. F. We cannot afford the pleasure of your society.

Liv. Let me assure you that I was ignorant of your misfortunes—and if I have not called—it was because—a—because—[*Aside.*] What shall I say. [*Aloud.*] I have been absent from the city ;—may I ask how is your sister ?

Paul. My sister Lucy is now employed in a millinery store in Broadway—she sees you pass the door every day.

Liv. [*Aside.*] The devil—I must confess my ruin, or appear a contemptible scoundrel.

Paul. Livingstone—I cannot conceal my feelings, we were schoolmates together—and I must speak out ——

Liv. [*Aside.*] I know what is coming.

Paul. I'm a blunt New York boy, and have something of the old bluff sailor's blood in my veins— so pardon me if I tell you that you have behaved badly to my sister Lucy.

Liv. For many months I was a daily visitor at your house—I loved your sister.

Paul. You asked me for Lucy's hand—I gave it, because I loved you as a brother—not because you were rich.

Liv. [*Aside.*] To retrieve my fortunes so that I might marry—I speculated in stocks and lost all I possessed. To enrich Lucy and her family I involved myself in utter ruin.

Paul. The next day I lost my clerkship—we were reduced to poverty, and you disappeared.

Liv. I can't stand it—I will confess all—let me sacrifice every feeling but Lucy's love and your esteem ——

Mrs. F. Beware, Mr. Livingstone, how you seek to renew our acquaintance : recollect my daughter earns a pittance behind a counter—I take in work, and Paul now seeks for the poorest means of earning an honest crust of bread.

Liv. And what would you say if I were no better off than yourselves—if I too were poor—if I——

Puffy. You, poor, you who own a square mile of New York ?

[*Enter* **Bloodgood.**]

Liv. Mr. Bloodgood !

Blood. Ah, Livingstone—why do you not call to see us ? You know our address—Madison Square—my daughter Alida will be delighted.—By the way—I have some paper of yours at the bank, it comes due to-day—ten thousand dollars, I think—you bank at the Chemical ?

Liv. Yes, I do—that is did,—bank there.

Blood. Why don't you bank with me, a rich and careless fellow like you—with a large account.

Liv. Yes—I—[*Aside.*] He is cutting the ground from under my feet.

Paul. Mr. Bloodgood—pardon me, sir, but I was about to call on you to-day to solicit employment.

Blood. I'm full, sir,—indeed I think of reducing salaries, everybody is doing so.

Liv. But you are making thousands a week !

Blood. That is no reason that I should not take advantage of the times—[*Recognizing* **Puffy**] Ah, Mr. Puffy, that note of yours.

Puffy. Oh, Lord ! [*Aside.*] It is the note Mrs. Fairweather gave me for her rent.

Blood. My patience is worn out.

Puffy. It's all right, sir.

Blood. Take care it is. [*Exit.*]

Puffy. There goes the hardest cuss that ever went to law.

Liv. Paul—my dear friend—will you believe me—my feelings are the same toward you—nay more tender, more sincere than ever—but there are circumstances I cannot explain.

Mrs. F. Mr. Livingstone, say no more—we ask no explanation.

Liv. But I ask something—let me visit you—let me return to the place that I once held in your hearts.

Puffy. 219 Division Street—Puffy, baker. Dinner at half-past one—come to-day, sir—do, sir.

Paul. We cannot refuse you.

Mrs. F. I will go to Lucy's store and let her know. Ah! Mr. Livingstone—she has never confessed that she loved you—but you will find her cheek paler than it used to be. [*Exit.*]

Paul. And now to hunt for work—to go from office to office pleading for employment—to be met always with the same answer—" we are full "—or " we are discharging hands "—Livingstone, I begin to envy the common laborer who has no fears, no care, beyond his food and shelter—I am beginning to lose my pity for the poor.

Liv. The poor!—whom do you call the poor? Do you know them? do you see them? they are more frequently found under a black coat than under a red shirt. The poor man is the clerk with a family, forced to maintain a decent suit of clothes, paid for out of the hunger of his children. The poor man is the artist who is obliged to pledge the tools of his trade to buy medicine for his sick wife. The lawyer who, craving for employment, buttons up his thin paletot to hide his shirtless breast. These needy wretches are poorer than the poor, for they are obliged to conceal their poverty with the false mask of content --smoking a cigar to disguise their hunger—they drag from their pockets their last quarter, to cast it with studied carelessness to the beggar, whose mattress at home is lined with gold. These are the most miserable of the Poor of New York. [*A small crowd has assembled round* **Livingstone** *during this speech ; they take him for an orator ; one of them takes down what he says on tablets.*]

[*Enter* **Policeman.**]

Puffy and crowd. Bravo—Bravo—Hurrah—get on the bench!

Police. Come—I say—this won't do.

Liv. What have I done?

Police. No stumping to the population allowed in the Park.

Liv. Stumping!

Reporter. Oblige me with your name, sir, for the Herald?

Liv. Oh! [*Rushes off, followed by* **Paul.**]

SCENE II.—*Exterior of* **Bloodgood's** *Bank, Nassau Street.*

[*Enter* **Bloodgood.**]

Blood. [*Looking at papers.*] Four per cent. a month—ha! if this panic do but last, I shall double my fortune! Twenty years ago this very month—ay, this very day—I stood in yonder bank a ruined man. Shall I never forget that night—when I and my accomplice carried out the body of the old sailor and laid it there! [*Points* L.] I never pass this spot without a shudder. But his money—that founded my new fortune. [*Enter* **Alida.**] Alida, my dear child what brings you to this part of the city?

Alida. I want two thousand dollars.

Blood. My dearest child, I gave you five hundred last week.

Alida. Pooh! what's five hundred? You made ten thousand in Michigan Southern last week—I heard you tell Mr. Jacob Little so.

Blood. But——

Alida. Come, don't stand fooling about it; go in and get the money—I must have it.

Blood. Well, my darling, if you must. Will you step in?

Alida. Not I. I'm not going into your dirty bank. I've seen all your clerks—they're not worth looking at.

Blood. I'll go and fetch it. [*Exit.*]

Alida. This is positively the last time I will submit to this extortion. [*Opens a letter and reads.*] " My adored Alida—I fly to your exquisite feet; I am the most wretched of men. Last night, at Hall's, I lost two thousand dollars—it must be paid before twelve o'clock. Oh, my queen! my angel! invent some excuse to get this money from your father, and meet me at Maillard's at half-past eleven. When shall we meet again alone, in that box at the opera, where I can press my lips to your superb eyes, and twine my hands in your magnificent hair? *Addio carissima!* THE DUKE OF CALCAVELLA." I wonder if he showed that to any of his friends before he sent it?

[*Re-enter* **Bloodgood,** *followed by* **Puffy.**]

Blood. I tell you, sir, it must be paid. I have given you plenty of time.

Puffy. You gave me the time necessary for you to obtain execution in the Marine Court.

Blood. Alida, my love, there is a draft for the money. [*Gives her notes. She takes them.*] And now you will do me a favor? Do not be seen about so much, in public, with that foreign duke.

Alida. I never ask you for a draft but you always give me a pill to take with it.

Blood. I don't like him.

Alida. I do—bye-bye. [*Exit.*]

Blood. How grand she looks! That girl possesses my whole heart.

Puffy. Reserve a little for me, sir. This here note, it was give to me by my second floor in payment of rent. It's as good as gold, sir—when they are able to pay it. I'd sooner have it——

Blood. Mr. Puffy, you are the worst kind of man ; you are a weak, honest fool, you are always failing—always the dupe of some new swindler.

Puffy. Lord love you, sir ! if you was to see the folks you call swindlers—the kindest, purest second floor as ever drew God's breath. I told them that this note was all right—for if they know'd I was put about along of it, I believe they'd sell the clothes off their backs to pay it.

Blood. [*Aside.*] This fellow is a fool. But I see, if I levy execution the note will be paid. [*Aloud.*] Very good, Mr. Puffy. I will see about it.

Puffy. You will ! I knew it—there—when folks says you're a hard man—I says—no—no more'n a rich man's got to be.

Blood. Very good. [*Aside.*] I'll put an execution on his house at once. [*Aloud.*] Good-morning, Mr. Puffy. [*Exit.*]

Puffy. Good-morning, sir. So, I'm floated off that mud bank. Lord ! if he had seized my goods and closed me up— I'd never a dared to look Mrs. Fairweather in the face agin. [*Exit.*]

SCENE III.—*The interior of* **Puffy's** *house. A poor but neat room—window at back.* **Mrs. Fairweather** *is arranging dinner.*

[*Enter* **Lucy,** *with a box.*]

Lucy. My dear mother.

Mrs. F. My darling Lucy. Ah, your eye is bright again. The thought of seeing Mark Livingstone has revived your smile.

Lucy. I have seen him. He and Paul called at Madame Victorine's.

Mrs. F. Is your work over, Lucy, already ?

Lucy. What we expected has arrived, mother. This dress is the last I shall receive from Madame Victorine--she is discharging her hands.

Mrs. F. More misfortunes—and Paul has not been able to obtain employment.

2

[Enter **Mrs. Puffy.***]*

Mrs. P. May I come in? It's only Mrs. Puffy. I've been over the oven for two hours! Knowing you had company—I've got a pigeon pie—such a pie!—um—oo—mutton kidneys in it —and hard biled eggs—love ye!—then I've got a chicken, done up a way of my own! I'll get on a clean gown and serve it up myself.

Mrs. F. But, my dear Mrs. Puffy—really we did not mean to incur any expense——

Mrs. P. Expense! why, wasn't them pigeons goin' to waste —they was shot by Dan—and we can't abide pigeons, neither Puffy nor I. Then the rooster was running round—always raisin' hereafter early in the mornin'—a noosance, it was——

[Enter **Dan.***]*

Dan. Beg pardon ladies—I just stepped in——
Lucy. Good-day, Dan.
Dan. Day, miss! *[Aside to* **Mrs. Puffy.***]* Oh! mother, ain't she pootty this mornin'?
Mrs. P. *[Smoothing her hair.]* What have you got there, Dan'el?
Dan. When I was paying the man for them birds—— *[***Mrs. P.** *kicks him.]* Creation! mother—you're like the stocks—you can't move a'thout crushin' somebody—well, he'd got this here pair o' boots ornder his arm—why, ses I, if ever dere was a foot created small enough to go into them, thar, it is Miss Lucy's— so I brought them for you to look at.
Lucy. They are too dear for me, Dan, pray give them back.
Dan. Well, ye see—the man has kinder gone, miss—he said he'd call again—some time next fall——
Mrs. F. Dan—Mrs. Puffy—you are good, kind, dear souls —when the friends of our better days have deserted us—when the rich will scarcely deign to remember us—you, without any design, but with the goodness of God in your hearts—without any hope but that of hiding your kindness, you help me. Give me your hands—I owe you too much already—but you must bestow on us no more out of your poverty.
Mrs. P. Lord, Mrs.! just as if me and Puffy could bestow anything—and what's Dan fit for?
Dan. Yes—what's I'm fit for?
Mrs. F. Well, I will accept your dinner to-day on one con-dition—that you will all dine with us.
Mrs. P. Oh—my! Dine with up-town folks!

Lucy. Yes indeed, Dan, you must.

Dan. Lord, miss! I ain't no account at dinin' with folks—I take my food on the fust pile of bricks, anyhow.

Mrs. P. I'm accustomed to mine standin', behind the counter.

Dan. We never set down to it, square out—except on Sundays.

Mrs. P. Then it don't seem natural—we never eat, each of us is employed a helping of the other.

Dan. I'll fix it! Father, and mother, and I, will all wait on you.

Lucy. [*Laughing.*] That's one way of dining together, certainly.

[*Enter* **Paul** *and* **Livingstone.**]

Liv. Here we are. Why, what a comfortable little cage this is!

Dan. Let me take your coat and hat, sir.

Liv. Thank you. [*Exit* **Dan** *and* **Mrs. Puffy.**] How like the old times, eh, Lucy? [*Sits by her.*]

Mrs. F. [*Aside to* **Paul.**] Well, Paul, have you obtained employment?

Paul. No, mother; but Livingstone is rich—he must have influence, and he will assist me.

Mrs. F. Heaven help us! I fear that the worst has not come.

Paul. Nonsense, mother—cheer up! Is there anything you have concealed from me?

Mrs. F. No—nothing you need know. [*Aside.*] If he knew that for five weeks we have been subsisting on the charity of these poor people!

[*Enter* **Mrs. Puffy** *with a pie, followed by* **Dan** *with a roast chicken, and* **Puffy**, *loaded with plates and various articles of dinner service.*]

Mrs. P. Here it is.

Lucy. Stay—we must lay more covers; help me, Paul.

Liv. Let me assist you. [*They join another table to the first.*]

Mrs. F. Mr. and Mrs. Puffy and Dan, dine with us.

Paul. Bravo!

Liv. Hail Columbia! [**Dan** *begins dancing about.*]

Lucy. Why, Dan—what's the matter?

Dan.   Oh, nothing, miss.

Lucy.   How red your face is!

Dan.   Don't mind, miss.

Mrs. P.   Oh, Lord! I forgot that dish; it has been in the oven for an hour.

Dan.   It ain't at all hot.   [**Paul** *touches it and jumps away.*] It's got to burn into the bone afore George Washington No. 4 gives in.   [*Lays down the plate—they all sit.*]

Puffy.   Now, this is agreeable—I have not felt so happy since I started my forty horse-power oven.

Liv.   This pie is magnificent.   [**Mrs. Puffy** *rises.*]

Mrs. P.   Oh, sir, you make me feel good.

Dan.   [*Holding the table.*]   Mother can't express her feelings without upsetting the table.

[*Enter two* **Sheriff's Officers.**]

Paul.   What persons are these?

Puffy.   What do you want?

First Sheriff's Officer.   I am the Deputy Sheriff—I come at the suit of Gideon Bloodgood, against Susan Fairweather and Jonas Puffy—amount of debt and costs, one hundred and fifty dollars.

Paul.   My mother!

Puffy.   He said he would see about it—Oh, Mrs. Fairweather —I hope you will forgive me—I couldn't help it.

Deputy Sheriff.   I do not want to distress you; Mr. Livingstone will perhaps pay the debt—or give me his check.

Paul.   Livingstone!

Liv.   [*After a pause.*]   I cannot help you.   Yes, I will rather appear what I am, a ruined man, than seem a contemptible one—I am penniless, broken—for weeks I have been so— but I never felt my poverty till now.

[*Tableau.*]

END OF ACT II.

ACT III.

SCENE.—*A room in the house of* **Gideon Bloodgood** ; *the furniture and ornaments are in a style of exaggerated richness —white satin and gold.*

Bloodgood *is discovered writing at a table on one side ;* **Alida** *seated, reading a newspaper, on the other.*]

Blood. What are you reading ?
Alida. The New York Herald.
Blood. You seem interested in it ?
Alida. Very.   Shall I read aloud ?
Blood. Do. [*Goes on writing.*]
Alida. [*Reads.*]   " Wall street is a perch, on which a row of human vultures sit, whetting their beaks, ready to fight over the carcass of a dying enterprise.   Amongst these birds of prey, the most vulturous is perhaps Gid. Bloodgood.   This popular financier made his fortune out of the lottery business.   He then dabbled a little in the slave trade, as the Paraquita case proved, —last week, by a speculation in flour, he made fifty thousand dollars ; this operation raised the price of bread four cents a loaf, and now there are a thousand people starving in the hovels of New York—we nominate Gid. for Congress, expenses to be paid by the admiring crowd—send round the hat." Father ! [*Rises.*] Are you not rich ?
Blood. Why do you ask ?
Alida. Because people say that riches are worshipped in New York, that wealth alone graduates society.   This is false, for I am young, handsome and your heiress—yet I am refused admission into the best families here whose intimacy I have sought.
Blood. Refused admission ! Is not Fifth Avenue open to you ?
Alida. Fifth Avenue ! that jest is stale.   Fifth Avenue is a shop where the richest fortunes are displayed like the dry goods in Stewart's windows, and like them, too, are changed daily. But why do we not visit those families at whose names all men and all journals bow with respect, the Livingstones, the Astors, the Van Renssalaers.   Father, these families receive men less rich than you—and honor many girls who don't dress as well as I do, nor keep a carriage.

Blood. Is not the Duke de Calcavella at your feet?

Alida. The Duke de Calcavella is an adventurer to whom you lend money, who escorts me to my box at the opera that he may get in free.

Blood. You minx, you know you love him.

Alida. I am not speaking of love—but of marriage.

Blood. Marriage!

Alida. Yes, marriage! This society in New York which has shut its doors against me, it is from amongst these families that I have resolved to choose a husband.

Blood. [*Rising.*] Alida, do you already yearn to leave me? For you alone I have hoarded my wealth—men have thought me miserly, when I have had but one treasure in the world, and that was you, my only child. To the rest of my fellow creatures I have been cold and calculating, because in you alone was buried all the love my heart could feel—my fortune, take it, gratify your caprices—take it all, but leave me your affection.

Alida. You talk as if I were still a child.

Blood. I would to God you were! Oh, Alida, if you knew how fearful a thing it is for a man like me to lose the only thing in the world that ties him to it!

Alida. Do you wish me to marry the Duke de Calcavella?

Blood. A *roué*, a gambler! Heaven forbid!

Alida. Besides, they say he has a wife in Italy.

Blood. I shall forbid him the house.

Alida. No, you won't.

Blood. His reputation will compromise yours.

Alida. Judge my nature by your own—I may blush from anger—never from shame.

[*Enter* **Edwards.**]

Edw. Mr. Mark Livingstone.

Alida. Livingstone! this is the first time that name has ever been announced in this house.

Blood. He comes on business. Tell Mr. Livingstone I cannot see him. Beg him to call at my office to-morrow.

Alida. Show him up.

Blood. Alida!

Alida. [*Sharply to* **Edwards.**] Do you hear me?

Blood. This is tyranny—I—I—[*In a rage to* **Edwards.**] Well, blockhead, why do you stand staring there? Don't you hear the order? Show him up. [*Exit* **Edwards.**]

Alida. Livingstone!

[*Enter* **Mark Livingstone.**]

Mark. Mr. Bloodgood—Miss Bloodgood—[*Bows.*] I am most fortunate to find you at home.

Alida. I trust that Mrs. Livingstone your mother, and Miss Livingstone your sister, are well?

Mark. [*Coldly.*] I thank you. [*Gaily.*] Allow me to assure you that you were the belle of the opera last night.

Alida. Yet you did not flatter me with your presence in our box.

Mark. You noticed my absence! you render me the happiest and proudest member of my club.

Alida. By the way, papa, I thought you were going to be a member of the Union.

Mark. Ahem! [*An awkward silence.*] He was black-balled last week.

Blood. I think, Mr. Livingstone, you have some business with me.

Alida. Am I in the way?

Mark. Not at all—the fact is, Miss Bloodgood—my business can be explained in three words.

Blood. Indeed!

Mark. I am ruined.

Alida. Ruined!

Mark. My father lived in those days when fancy stocks were unknown, and consequently was in a position to leave me a handsome fortune. I spent it—extravagantly—foolishly. My mother, who loves me "not wisely but too well," heard that my name was pledged for a large amount,—Mr. Bloodgood held my paper—she sold out all her fortune without my knowledge, and rescued my credit from dishonor.

Blood. Allow me to observe, I think she acted honorably, but foolishly.

Mark. [*Bows to* **Bloodgood.**] She shared my father's ideas on these matters; well [*turns to* **Alida,**] finding I was such good pay, your father lent me a further sum of money, with which I speculated in stocks to recover my mother's loss—I bulled the market—lost—borrowed more—the crisis came—I lost again—until I found myself ruined.

Blood. [*Rising.*] Mr. Livingstone, I anticipate the object of your present visit—you desire some accommodation—I regret that it is out of my power to accord it. If you had applied to me a few days earlier I might have been able to——but—a— at the present moment it is quite impossible.

Mark. [*Aside.*] Impossible—the usual expression—I am familiar with it. [*Rising—aloud.*] I regret exceedingly that I did not fall on that more fortunate moment to which you allude—a thousand pardons for my untimely demand——

Blood. I hope you believe that I am sincere when I say——

Mark. Oh! I am sure of it. Accept my thanks—good-morning, Miss Bloodgood.

Blood. [*Ringing the bell.*] I trust you will not be put to serious inconvenience.

Mark. Oh, no. [*Aside.*] A revolver will relieve me of every difficulty. [*Aloud.*] Good-day, Mr. Bloodgood. [*Exit.*]

Blood. I like his impudence! To come to me for assistance! Let him seek it of his aristocratic friends—his club associates who black-balled me last week.

Alida. [*Who has been seated writing at table.*] Father, come here.

Blood. What is it?

Alida. I am writing a letter which I wish you to sign.

Blood. To whom?

Alida. To Mr. Livingstone.

Blood. To Livingstone!

Alida. Read it.

Blood. [*Reads.*] "My dear sir, give yourself no further anxiety about your debt to me; I will see that your notes are paid—and if the loan of ten thousand dollars will serve you, I beg to hold that amount at your service, to be repaid at your convenience. Yours, truly." [*Throwing down letter.*] I will write nothing of the kind.

Alida. You are mistaken—you will write nothing else.

Blood. With what object?

Alida. I want to make a purchase.

Blood. Of what?

Alida. Of a husband—a husband who is a gentleman—and through whom I can gain that position you cannot with all your wealth obtain—you see—the thing is cheap—there's the pen. [*She rings a bell.*]

Blood. Is your mind so set on this ambition?

Alida. If it cost half your fortune. [**Bloodgood** *signs. Enter* **Edwards.** *To servant.*] Deliver this letter immediately.

Edw. [*Takes the letter and is going out, when he runs against* **Badger,** *who is coolly entering.*] I have told you already that my master is not to be seen.

Bad. So you did—but you see how mistaken you were. There he is—I can see him distinctly.

Blood. Badger ! [*To* **Edwards.**] You may go, Edwards.

Bad. [*To* **Edwards.**] James—get out.

Blood. What can he want here ?

Bad. Respected Gideon, excuse my not calling more promptly, but since my return from California, this is my first appearance in fashionable society.

Alida. [*Proudly.*] Who is this fellow ?

Bad. Ah, Alida, how is the little tootles ? You forget me.

Alida. How can I recollect every begging imposter who importunes my father.

Bad. Charming ! The same as ever—changed in form—but the heart, my dear Gideon, the same as ever, is hard and dry as a biscuit.

Alida. Father, give this wretch a dollar and let him go.

Bad. Hullo ! Miss Bloodgood, when I hand round the hat it is time enough to put something in it. Gideon, ring and send that girl of yours to her nurse.

Alida. Is this fellow mad ?

Blood. Hush ! my dear !

Alida. Speak out your business—I am familiar with all my father's affairs.

Bad. All ? I doubt it.

[*Enter* **Edwards,** *followed by* **Lucy.**]

Edw. This way, Miss. [*To* **Alida.**] Here is your dress-maker.

Alida. [*Eyeing* **Lucy.**] Ha ! you are the young person I met this morning walking with Mr. Livingstone ?

Lucy. Yes, madam.

Alida. Hum ! follow me, and let me see if you can attend on ladies as diligently as you do on gentlemen. [*Exeunt* **Alida** *and* **Lucy.**]

Blood. [*Looking inquiringly at* **Badger.**] So you are here again. I thought you were dead.

Bad. No ; here I am—like a bad shilling, come back again. I've been all over the world since we parted twenty years ago. Your $3,000 lasted me for some months in California. Believe me, had I known that, instead of absconding, you remained in New York, I would have hastened back again ten years ago, to share your revived fortunes.

Blood. I am at a loss to understand your allusions, sir,— nor do I know the object of your return to this city. We have plenty of such persons as you in New York.

Bad. The merchants of San Francisco did not think so, for they subscribed to send me home.

Blood. What do you mean?

Bad. I mean the Vigilance Committee.

Blood. And what do you intend to do here?

Bad. Reduced in circumstances and without character, the only resource left to me is to start a bank.

Blood. Well, Mr. Badger; I cannot see in what way these things can affect me!

Bad. Can't you? Ahem! Do you ever read the Sunday papers?

Blood. Never.

Bad. I've got a romance ready for one of them—allow me to give you a sketch of it.

Blood. Sir——

Bad. The scene opens in a bank in Nassau Street. Twenty years ago a very respectable old sea captain, one winter's night, makes a special deposit of one hundred thousand dollars—nobody present but the banker and one clerk. The old captain takes a receipt and goes on his way rejoicing—but, lo! and behold you!—in half an hour he returns—having ascertained a fact or two, he demands his money back, but while receiving it he is seized by a fit of apoplexy, and he dies on the spot. End of Chapter One.

Blood. Indeed, Mr. Badger, your romance is quite original.

Bad. Ain't it! never heard it before, did you?—no! Good! Chapter Two. [*Pointedly.*] The banker and his clerk carried the body out on the sidewalk, where it was discovered, and the next day the Coroner's Jury returned a verdict accordingly. The clerk receiving $3,000 hush money left for parts unknown. The banker remained in New York, and on the profits of this plunder established a colossal fortune. End of Part No. 1—to be continued in our next.

Blood. And what do you suppose such a romance will be worth?

Bad. I've come to you to know.

Blood. I am no judge of that.

Bad. Ain't you?—well—in Part No. 2, I propose to relate that this history is true in every particular, and I shall advertise for the heirs of the dead man.

Blood. Ha! you know his name then?

Bad. Yes, but I see you don't. I wrote the acknowledgment which you signed—you had not even the curiosity then to read the name of your victim.

Blood. Really, Mr. Badger, I am at a loss to understand you. Do you mean to insinuate that this romance applies in any way to me?

Bad. It has a distant reference.

Blood. Your memory is luxurious—perhaps it can furnish some better evidence of this wonderful story than the word of a convict ejected from California as a precaution of public safety.

Bad. You are right—my word is not worth much.

Blood. I fear not.

Bad. But the receipt, signed by you, is worth a good deal.

Blood. [*Starting.*] Ha! you lie!

Bad. Let us proceed with my romance. When the banker and his clerk searched for the receipt, they could not find it—a circumstance which only astonished one of the villains—because the clerk had picked up the document and secured it in his pocket. I don't mean to insinuate that this applies in any way to you.

Blood. Villain!

Bad. Moral: As a general rule, never destroy receipts—it is no knowing when they may not prove useful.

Blood. Were it so, this receipt is of no value in your hands —the heirs of the dead man can alone establish a claim.

Bad. [*Rising.*] That's the point—calculate the chance of my finding them, and let me know what it is worth.

Blood. What do you demand?

Bad. Five thousand dollars.

Blood. Five thousand devils!

Bad. You refuse?

Blood. I defy you—find the heir if you can.

[*Enter* Edwards.]

Edw. Mr. Paul Fairweather!

[*Enter* Paul. Badger *starts, then falls laughing in a chair.*]

Blood. Your business, sir, with me.

Paul. Oh, pardon me, Mr. Bloodgood—but the officers have seized the furniture of our landlord—of your tenant—for a debt owed by my mother. I come to ask your mercy—utter ruin awaits two poor families.

Bad. Oh, Supreme Justice! there is the creditor, and there is the debtor.

Paul. My mother—my sister—I plead for them, not for myself.

Blood. I have waited long enough.

Bad. [*Rising.*] So have I. [*To* **Paul.**] Have you no friends or relations to help you ?

Paul. None, sir ; my father is dead. [**Bloodgood** *returns to his table.*]

Blood. Enough of this. [*Rings the bell.*]

Bad. Not quite ; I feel interested in this young gentleman— don't you ?

Blood. Not at all ; therefore my servant will show you both out—so you may talk this matter over elsewhere.

Bad. [*To* **Paul.**] Your name is familiar to me—was your father in trade ?

Paul. He was a sea captain.

Bad. Ah ! he died nobly in some storm, I suppose—the last to leave his ship ?

Paul. No, sir, he died miserably ! ten years ago, his body was found on the sidewalk in Liberty Street, where he fell dead by apoplexy.

Blood. [*Rising.*] Ah !

[*Enter* **Edwards.**]

Bad. James, show us out—we'll talk over this matter elsewhere.

Blood. No—you—you can remain. Leave us, Edwards.

Bad. Ah, I told you that the young man was quite interesting. Alphonse, get out. [*Exit* **Edwards.**]

Blood. My dear Mr. Badger, I think we have a little business to settle together ?

Bad. Yes, my dear Gideon. [*Aside to him.*] Stocks have gone up—I want fifty thousand dollars for that receipt.

Blood. Fifty thousand !

Bad. [*Aside.*] You see the effect of good news on the market—quite astounding ; ain't it ?

Blood. If you will step down to the dining-room, you will find lunch prepared—refresh yourself, while I see what can be done for this young man.

Bad. [*Aside.*] What are you up to ? You want to fix him —to try some game to euchre me. Go it ! I've got the receipt ; you're on the hook—take out all the line you want. [*Calls.*] Ho ! without there ! [*Enter* **Edwards.**] Maximilian, vamos ! Show me to the banquetting-hall. [*Exit, with* **Edwards.**]

Blood. Your situation interests me ; but surely, at your age —you can find employment.

Paul. Alas, sir, in these times, it is impossible. I would work, yes, at any kind of labor—submit to anything, if I could save my mother and my sister from want.

Blood. Control your feelings : perhaps I can aid you.

Paul. Oh, sir, I little expected to find in you a benefactor.

Blood. My correspondents at Rio Janeiro require a bookkeeper—are you prepared to accept this situation ? but there is a condition attached to this employment that may not suit you —you must start by the vessel which sails to-morrow.

Paul. To-morrow !

Blood. I will hand you a thousand dollars in advance of salary, to provide for your mother and sister ; they had better leave the city until they can follow you. You hesitate !

Paul. Oh, sir, 'tis my gratitude that renders me silent.

Blood. You accept ? the terms are two thousand dollars a year.

Paul. [*Seizing his hand.*] Mr. Bloodgood, the prayers of a family, whom you have made happy, will prosper your life. God bless you, sir ! I speak not for myself, but those still more dear to me.

Blood. Call again in an hour, when your papers of introduction and the money shall be ready.

Paul. Farewell, sir. I can scarcely believe my good fortune. [*Exit.*]

Blood. So, now to secure Badger. [*Sitting down and writing.*] He must, at any risk, be prevented from communicating with the mother and daughter until they can be sent into some obscure retreat. I doubt that he is in possession of this receipt, [*rings a bell*] but I will take an assurance about that. [*Rings.*] [*Enter* **Edwards.**] Take this letter instantly to the office of the Superintendent of Police. [*Exit* **Edwards.**] Ha ! Badger, when you find the heirs of the estate gone, you will perhaps come down in your terms. You did not remain long enough in California to measure wits with Gideon Bloodgood. [*Exit.*]

[*Enter* **Lucy.**]

Lucy. I will do my best, miss, to please you. Oh, let me hasten from this house !

[*Enter* **Mark Livingstone.**]

Mark. Lucy !

Lucy. Mark !

Mark. What brings you here ?

Lucy. What brings the poor into the saloons of the rich ?

[Enter Alida, unseen by the others.]

Alida. *[Aside.]* Mr. Livingstone here, and with this girl !

Mark. My dear Lucy, I have news, bright news, that will light up a smile in your eyes—I am once more rich. But before I relate my good fortune, let me hear from you the consent to share it.

Lucy. What do you mean ?

Mark. I mean, dearest one, that I love you—I love you with all my reckless, foolish, worthless heart.

Alida. *[Advancing.]* Mr. Livingstone, my father is waiting for you in his study.

Mark. A thousand pardons, Miss Bloodgood ; I was not aware—excuse me. *[Aside.]* I wonder if she overheard me. *[To Lucy.]* I will see you again this evening. *[Exit.]*

Alida. *[To Lucy, who is going.]* Stay ; one word with you. Mr. Livingstone loves you ! do not deny it, I have overheard you.

Lucy. Well, Miss Bloodgood, I have no account to render you in this matter.

Alida. I beg your pardon—he is to be my husband.

Lucy. Your husband ?

Alida. Be quiet and listen. Mr. Livingstone is ruined—my father has come to his aid ; but one word from me, and the hand, extended to save him from destruction, will be withdrawn.

Lucy. But you will not speak that word ?

Alida. That depends——

Lucy. On what, his acceptance of your hand ? He does not love you.

Alida. That is not the question.

Lucy. You have overheard that he loves *me*.

Alida. That is no concern of mine.

Lucy. And you will coldly buy this man for a husband, knowing that you condemn him to eternal misery !

Alida. You are candid, but not complimentary. Let us hope that in time he will forget you, and learn to endure me.

Lucy. Oh, you do not love him. I see, it is his name you require to cover the shame which stains your father's, and which all his wealth cannot conceal. Thank Heaven ! his love for me will preserve him from such a cowardly scheme.

Alida. I will make him rich. What would you make him ?

Lucy. I would make him happy.

Alida. Will you give him up ?

Lucy. Never!

Alida. Be it so.

[*Re-enter* **Mark.**]

Mark. Lucy, dear Lucy, do you see that lady?—she is my guardian angel. To her I owe my good fortune—Mr. Bloodgood has told me all, and see, this letter is in her own handwriting; now, let me confess, Miss Bloodgood, that had I not been thus rescued from ruin, I had no other resource but a Colt's revolver.

Lucy. Mark!

Mark. Yes, Lucy—I had resolved I could not endure the shame and despair which beset me on all sides. But let us not talk of such madness—let us only remember that I owe her my life.

Alida. [*Aside.*] And I intend to claim the debt.

Mark. More than my life—I owe to her all that happiness which you will bestow upon me.

Lucy. Me! me!—Mark!—No, it is impossible.

Mark. Impossible!

Lucy. I cannot be your wife.

Mark. What mean you, Lucy?

Lucy. [*With a supreme effort.*] I—I do not love you.

Mark. You jest, Lucy—yet, no—there are tears in your eyes.

Lucy. [*Looking away.*] Did I ever tell you that I loved you?

Mark. No, it is true—but your manner, your looks, I thought——

Lucy. You are not angry with me, are you?

Mark. I love you too sincerely for that, and believe me I will never intrude again on your family, where my presence now can only produce pain and restraint; may I hope, however, that you will retain enough kindness towards me as to persuade your mother to accept my friendship? It will soothe the anguish you have innocently inflicted, if your family will permit me to assist them. Have you the generosity to make this atonement? I know it will pain you all—but you owe it to me. [**Lucy** *falls, weeping, in a chair.*] Pardon me, Miss Bloodgood. Farewell, Lucy. [*To* **Alida.**] I take my leave. [*Exit.*]

Alida. He has gone—you may dry your eyes.

Lucy. Oh! I know what starvation is—I have met want face to face, and I have saved him from that terrible extremity.

Alida. He offered you money ; I should prefer that my husband should not have pecuniary relations with you—at least, not at present—so, as you are in want—here is some assistance. [*Offers her purse to* **Lucy.**]

Lucy. [*Rising.*] You insult me, Miss Bloodgood.

Alida. How can an offer of money insult anybody ?

Lucy. You thought I sold my heart—no—I gave it. Keep your gold, it would soil my poverty ; you have made two fellow-beings unhappy for life—God forgive you ! [*Exit.*]

[*Re-enter* **Bloodgood.**]

Blood. What is the matter, Alida ?

[*Re-enter* **Badger.**]

Bad. Your cook is perfect, your wine choice. [*He pockets the napkin.*] Well, now suppose we do a little business.

Blood. [*Rings bell.*] It is time we began to understand each other. [*Enter* **Edwards.**] Has that letter been delivered ? [**Edwards** *bows, and at a sign from* **Bloodgood.** *exit.*]

Bad. Do you wish to enter into particulars in the presence of this charming creature ?

Blood. Her presence will not affect our business.

[*Re-enter* **Edwards**, *and two* **Police Officers.**]

Bad. Just as you please. What proposition have you to make ?

Blood. I propose to give you into custody for an attempt to extort money by threats and intimidation.

First Pol. You are our prisoner.

Bad. Arrested !

Blood. Let him be searched ; on his person will be found a receipt signed by me, which he purloined from my desk yonder.

Bad. Well played, my dear Gideon, but, knowing the character of the society into which I was venturing, I left the dear document safe at home. Good-morning, Gid—Miss Bloodgood, yours. General—Colonel—take care of me. [*Goes up with* **Policemen.**]

END OF ACT III.

ACT IV.

SCENE I.—*Union Square—Night. The snow falls.*

[**Puffy** *discovered*, R. H. *with a pan of roasting chestnuts.*
Paul *crouches in a corner of the street.*]

Puffy. Lord! how cold it is. I can't sell my chestnuts. I thought if I posted myself just here, so as to catch the grand folks as they go to the opera, they might fancy to take in a pocketful, to eat during the performance.

[*Enter* **Dan**, *with two trunks on his shoulders, followed by a* **Gentleman.**]

Dan. There is the hotel. I'll wait here while you see if you can get a room. [*Exit* **Gentleman**, *into hotel.*]

Puffy. Dan, my boy, what cheer?

Dan. This is the fust job I've had to-day.

Puffy. I've not taken a cent.

Dan. Have you been home to dinner?

Puffy. No ; I took a chestnut. There wasn't more than enough for the old woman and you, so I dined out.

Dan. I wasn't hungry much, so I borried a bit o' 'bacca.

Puffy. Then the old woman had all the dinner, that's some comfort—one of us had a good meal to-day.

Dan. I don't know, father—she's just ugly enough to go and put it by for our supper.

[*Enter* **Mrs. Puffy**, *with a tin can.*]

Puffy. Here she is.

Mrs. P. Ain't you a nice pair? For five mortal hours I've been carryin' this dinner up and down Broadway.

Dan. I told you so.

Mrs. P. You thought to give old mother the slip, you un-dootiful villin—but I've found ye both. Come, here's your suppers—I've kept it warm under my cloak.

Puffy. Lay the table on the gentleman's trunk.

Dan. [*Looking into the tin can.*] A splendid lump of bread, and a chunk of beef!

Puffy. Small feed for three human beings.

Dan. Here goes.

Puffy. Stay, Dan. [*Placing his hands over the bread.*] God bless us, and pity the Poor of New York. Now, I'll share the food in three.

3

Dan. [*Pointing to* **Paul.**] Father, that cuss in the corner there looks kinder bad—suppose you have the food in four.

Mrs. P. I don't want none. Give him mine—I ain't at all cold.

Dan. Mother, there's a tear on the end of your nose—let me break it off. ·

Mrs. P. Get out.

Dan. [*Takes a piece of bread, and goes to* **Paul.**] Hello, stranger! He's asleep.

Mrs. P. Then don't wake him. Leave the bread in his lap. [**Dan** *places the bread, softly, beside* **Paul,** *and rejoins the party —they eat.*]

[*Enter a* **Gentleman,** *followed by* **Badger.**]

Bad. [*Very ragged, with some opera books in one hand, and boxes of matches in the other.*] Book of the opera slr? take a book, sir—they will charge you double inside. Well, buy a box of lucifers—a hundred for three cents. [*Dodging in front of him to prevent him passing.*] Genuine Pollak's—try one. [*Exit* **Gentleman**—**Badger** *changes his tone, and calls after him.*] If you're short of cash, I'll lend you a shilling. He wants all he has got to pay his omnibus. Jerusha! ain't it cold! Tum-iddy-tum-iddy-tum. [*Performs a short dance, while he hums a banjo melody.*] I could play the banjo on my stomach, while all my shivering anatomy would supply the bones.

[*Enter* **Mrs. Fairweather.**]

Mrs. F. I cannot return to our miserable home without food for my children. Each morning we separate in search of work, in search of food, only to meet again at night—their poor faces thin with hunger. [*She clasps her hands in anguish.*] Ah! what's here? yes, this remains—it is gold!

Bad. [*Overhearing her last word.*] Gold! Book of the opera, ma'am?

Mrs. F. Tell me, friend, where can I buy a loaf of bread at this hour?

Bad. There's a saloon open in the Fourth Avenue. [*Aside.*] Gold—she said gold.

Mrs. F. Will they accept this pledge for some food? [*Shows a ring to* **Badger.**]

Bad. [*Eagerly.*] Let me see it. [*Looks round.*]

Mrs. F. It is my wedding ring. [**Badger** *examines it by the light of the druggist's window.*]

Bad. [*Aside.*] I can easily make off with it. [*Rubs his nose with the ring while he considers.*]

Mrs. F. My children are starving—I must part with it to buy them bread.

Bad. [*Whistles—hesitates—and returns the ring.*] Go along, go ; buy your children food, start, and don't show that ring to anybody else. You deserve to lose it for showing it to such a blackguard as I am. [*Exit* **Mrs. Fairweather.**]

[*Enter* **Bloodgood.**]

Blood. What's the time. The opera must be nearly over. [*Looks at his watch by the light of the druggist's window.*]

Bad. Book of the opera, sir—only authorized edition. [*Recognizing him.*] Bloodgood !

Blood. Badger ! [*They advance.* **Bloodgood** *puts his hand into the breast of his coat.*]

Bad. Ah, my dear Gideon—— [*Suddenly.*] Take your hand out of your breast—come ! none of that—I've a knife up my sleeve that would rip you up like a dried codfish before you could cock that revolver you have there so handy.

Blood. [*Withdrawing his hand.*] You are mistaken.

Bad. Oh, no ! I am not. I have not been ten years in California for nothing—you were just thinking that you could blow out my brains, and swear that I was trying to garrote you.

Blood. What do you want ?

Bad. I want your life—but legally. A week ago, I came out of prison—you had removed the Fairweather family—I could not find a trace of them but I found the receipt where I had concealed it. To-morrow I shall place it in the hands of the District Attorney with my confession of our murder of the sea captain.

Blood. Murder——

Bad. Only think what a fine wood-cut for the Police Gazette we shall make, carrying out the dead body between us.

Blood. Demon !

Bad. There will be a correct plan of your back office in the Herald—headed—the Bloodgood Tragedy.

Blood. Come to my house to-morrow, and bring that document with you.

Bad. No, sir—ee ! once caught twice shy. You owe me a call. Come to my house, to-night—and alone.

Blood. Where do you live ?

Bad. Nineteen and a half Cross Street, Five Points—fifth floor back—my name is on the door in chalk.

Blood. In an hour I will be there.

Bad. In an hour. Don't forget to present my compliments to your charming daughter--sweet creature! the image of her father--how I should like to write something in her album. [*Exit* **Bloodgood.** *Enter two* **Gentlemen** *from hotel—they talk. Cries.*] Here's lucifers--three cents a hundred. [**Gentlemen** *shake hands and separate. Following one off.*] Here's this miscellaneous stock of lumber, just imported from Germany, to be sold out--an alarming sacrifice, in consequence of the present state of the money market. [*Exit importuning the* **Gentleman,** *who tries to escape.*]

Puffy. Come, mother, we must get home.

Mrs. P Dan, have you seen nothing of poor Mrs. Fairweather and her children? ·

Dan. No, mother--I can't find out where they have gone to --I guess they've quit New York.

Mrs. P. God help them—wherever they are!

Puffy. Come, mother. [*Music—***Puffy** *and* **Mrs. P.** *go out —***Dan** *goes up and speaks with* **Gentleman.**]

[*Enter* **Lucy.**]

Lucy. This is the place. The Sisters of Charity in Houston street told me that I might find work at this address. [*Reads paper.*] Fourteenth Street. Oh, Heaven! be merciful to me, this is my last hope. [*Exit.*]

[**Paul** *rises and comes forward.*]

Paul. My limbs are powerless. How long have I slept there?—another long day has passed—I have crept round the hotels—the wharves—I have begged for work—but they laughed at my poor, thin form—the remnant of better days hung in tatters about me—and I was thrust from the door by stronger wretches than I. To-day I applied to get employment as a waiter in a hotel--but no, I looked too miserable. Oh, my mother! my poor mother! my dear sister! were it not for you, I would lie down here and die where I was born, in the streets of New York.

Dan. All right, sir—to the Brevoort House. Here, you lazy cuss, shoulder this trunk, and earn a quarter——

[*Enter a* **Porter.**]

Paul. Yes -oh, gladly!

Porter. It's myself will do that same. [**Paul** *and the* **Porter**

seize the trunk.] Lave yer hoult—you dandy chap wid the black coat.

Paul. He called to me.

Porter. Is it the likes of you—that ud be takin' the bread out of the mouths of honest folks.

Paul. God help me! I have not tasted bread for two days.

Porter. The Lord save us! why didn't ye say so?—take the trunk and welkim. [**Paul** *trying to lift it. Exit* **Dan.**]

Gent. Come along, quick! [*Exit* **Gentleman.**]

Paul. [*Unable to lift it, staggers back.*] I—I—can't—I am too weak from hunger.

Porter. Look at this, my jewel. [*Tossing the trunk on his shoulder.*] That's the way of it—all right, yer honor. [*Exit* **Porter.**]

Paul. [*Falling against the lamp-post in despair, on his knees.*] Oh, God!—you who have refused to me the force to earn my bread, give me the resignation to bear your will.

[*Re-enter* **Lucy.**]

Lucy. The lady was from home—they told me to call next week—oh, could I see some kindly face—I would beg, yes—I would ask alms. [*Enter a* **Gentleman.**] Sir—pardon me—would you——

Gent. Eh?

Lucy. [*Stammering.*] I—I—I——

Gent. What do you want?

Lucy. [*Faintly.*] The—the—Bowery—if—if—you please——

Gent. Just turn to the right, and keep straight on. [*Exit.*]

Lucy. Oh, coward! coward!—I have not the courage to beg.

[*Enter* **Mrs. Fairweather.**]

Mrs. F. They refused to take my ring—they said I had stolen it—They drove me from the house. To what have I come!—to beg in the streets—yes, for them, for my children!

Paul. [*Rising.*] Let me return to our home—perhaps mother or Lucy may have found work.

Mrs. F. Sir! sir!—In the name of your mother—help my poor children.

Lucy. [*Covering her face with one hand, and holding out the other.*] For pity's sake—give me the price of——

Paul. Mother!
Lucy. My brother! } [*Together.*]
Mrs. F. My son!

Paul. Oh, mother! my own Lucy! my heart is broken. [*They embrace.*] Have you concealed from me the extent of your misery?

Mrs. F. My son! my poor children! I cannot see you die of hunger and cold!

Paul. Take Lucy home, mother—and I will bring you food!

Mrs. F. Paul, promise me that nothing will tempt you to a dishonorable act.

Paul. Do not fear, mother; the wretched have always one resource—they can die! Do not weep, Lucy—in an hour I will be with you. [*Exeunt* **Lucy** *and* **Mrs. Fairweather**] I will go and await the crowd as they leave the Academy of Music —amongst them Heaven will inspire some Christian heart to aid me. [*Exit.*]

SCENE II.—*The vestibule of the Academy of Music.*

[*Enter* **Alida** *and* **Livingstone.** *Music within.*]

Alida. How strange that my father has not returned.

Mark. Allow me to look for the carriage.

Alida. I will remain here. [*Exit* **Livingstone.**] At last I have won the husband I desire. He is entangled in my father's debt: in one month hence I shall be Livingstone's wife. Our box is now crowded with the first people in New York.—The dear Duke still makes love to me—to which Livingstone appears indifferent—so much the better—once Mrs. Livingstone he may do as he likes and so will I.

[*Enter* **Paul.**]

Paul. Ah! 'tis she—Alida Bloodgood.

Alida. I wonder they permit such vagabonds to hang about the opera.

[*Re-enter* **Livingstone.**]

Mark. The carriage is ready—[*Recognizing* **Paul.**] Paul!

Paul. Livingstone!

Mark. Great heaven! In what a condition do I find you?

Paul. We are poor—we are starving.

Alida. Give the fellow a dollar, and send him away.

Mark. My dear Alida, you do not know—this is a schoolfellow—an old friend——

Alida. I know that you are keeping me in the cold—ah! I see the Duke of Calcavella on the steps yonder, smoking a cigar. He will see me home, don't let me take you from your old friend. [*Exit.*]

Mark. [*Aside.*] Cold—heartless girl! [*Aloud.*] Come, Paul, come quickly, bring me to where I shall find your mother —your sister—stay, let me first go home and get money, I will meet you at your lodgings—where do you live?

Paul. Number nineteen and a half Cross Street—Five Points —I will wait for you at the door.

Mark. In less than an hour I shall be there. [*Exeunt.*]

SCENE III.—*No.* 19½ *Cross Street—Five Points. Two adjoining attic rooms. That of* **Badger,** L. H. *That of the* **Fairweather** *family,* R. H. *Music.* **Lucy** *is seated* C. *and* **Mrs. Fairweather** *kneels* R.]

Lucy. Surely an hour has passed and Paul has not returned.

Mrs. F. Oh, merciful father! protect my poor children.

[*Enter* **Badger** *in his attic* R. H. *with his box of matches. He scrapes several which do not light.* **Mrs. Fairweather** *rises and goes to window.*]

Bad. One hundred matches like that for one cent. [*Lighting one.*] Oh, lucky chance! Here's one that condescends. [*Lights a candle in a bottle.*]

Mrs. F. Day after day goes by—no hope—the future worse than the present—dark—dark. Oh! this load of wretchedness is too much to bear?

Lucy. The candle is going out.

Mrs. F. So much the better, I shall not be able to see your tears. [**Lucy** *rests her face on her hands.*]

Bad. [*Taking a bottle from his pocket.*] There's the concentrated essence of comfort—the poor man's plaster for the inside.

Lucy. [*Aside.*] Is there no way to end this misery? None but death!

Bad. [*Taking from pocket a slice of bread and meat wrapped in a bit of newspaper.*] Here's my supper. [*Addressing an imaginary servant.*] James, lay the table—spread the tablecloth.—Yes, sa!—[*Places the newspaper over the table.*] It's cold here, there's a draught in this room, some-where.—James, champagne. Thank you, James. [*Drinks and eats.*]

Mrs. F. [*Aside, coming down* R.] If Paul had only Lucy to support, they might live—why should I prolong my life only to hasten theirs.

Bad. The draught comes from—[*examining the wall*]—yes there are great chinks in the wall—I must see my landlord and solicit repairs.   A new family moved into the next room, yesterday ; I wonder who they are ?

Lucy.   The wretched always have one resource—they can die !

Bad.   [*At his table eating—he has taken the blanket from his bed and wrapped it about his shoulders.*]   Now let us do a little business.   James, turn up the gas.   Yes, sa !—[*He snuffs the candle with his fingers.*]   Thank you.   Ahem ! James Bloodgood is coming for the receipt bequeathed to me by the old sailor.   What price shall we set upon it, James ?

Lucy.   [*Aside.*]   When I am gone, there will be one mouth less to feed—Paul will have but one care to provide for.

Mrs. F.   [*Aside.*]   In this room, we had some charcoal— there is enough left to bestow on me an easy death.   [**Mrs. Fairweather** *exits by door* R. H.]

Bad.   I think $50,000 would be the figure—Oh, what a prospect opens before me—50,000 dollars—I should resume specie payments.

Lucy.   [*Looks into* R. H. *room.*]   What is mother doing ! ah, she is lighting the pan of charcoal on which we prepare our food—ah !—the thought !—could I induce her to leave me alone. Hem.—The deadly fumes of that fuel will bestow on me an easy death.

Mrs. F.   [*Re-enters.*]   It is there—now, now, while I have the courage of despair.

Bad.   50,000 dollars !   I'll have a pair of fast trotters, and dine at Delmonico's.   James, more champagne.   [*Takes a drink from bottle.*]   Thank you——

Lucy *and* **Mrs. F.**   [*Together.*]   Mother—Lucy.

Lucy.   Dear mother—I have just thought of a friend—a—a —fellow work girl, from whom I may get assistance——

Mrs. F.   Go, then, my child—yes—go at once.

Lucy.   I fear to go alone.   Come with me, you can wait at the corner of the street until I come out.

Mrs. F.   [*Putting on her bonnet. Aside.*]   When she is out of sight, I can return and accomplish my purpose.

Lucy.   [*Casting a cloak over her head. Aside.*]   I will come back by another way.

Mrs. F.   Come, Lucy.

Lucy.   I am ready, mother.   [*Aside.*]   She does not think that we are about to part forever.

Mrs. F.   [*Aside.*]   My poor child !

Lucy.   Kiss me—mother, for my heart is cold.   [*They embrace.*]

Bad. [*Cogitating.*] 50,000 dollars ! I'll have a box at Grace Church and a pew at the opera.

Lucy. Mother, I am ready. [*Exeunt.*]

Bad. [*Finding his bottle empty.*] What's the news ? Let us consult my tablecloth. What journal have we here. [*Reads.*] "Chevalier Greely has got a new hat."—It's the Herald—What's here ?—[*Reads.*] " You lie—villainy—you lie, and you know it." No ! it's the Tribune.

[*Enter* **Bloodgood.**]

Blood. Ah, Mr. Badger.

Bad. Please to wipe your feet before you come in—my carpet is new. I am glad to see you. Take a seat upon the sofa. [*Pointing to bed.*]

Blood. Come, sir ; to business. You have the receipt with you, I suppose ?

Bad. You know I've got it, or you would not have come.

Blood. How much do you want for it ?

Bad. Stay a moment. Let us see. You have had for twenty years in your possession the sum of $100,000, the profits of one robbery—well, at 8 per cent., this sum would now be doubled.

Blood. Let me see the document, and then we can estimate its value.

Bad. [*Drawing receipt from pocket.*] Here it is.

Blood. [*Springing towards him.*] Let me have it.

Bad. Hands off !

Blood. [*Drawing pistol.*] That paper, give it me, or I'll blow your brains out !

Bad. [*Edging slowly towards the bed.*] Ah ! that's your calculation.

Blood. Now you are in my power.

Bad. It's an old dodge, but ineffective. Come, no violence —I'll give you the paper.

Blood. A bullet is good argument.

Bad. [*Drawing from beneath his pillow two enormous pistols.*] A brace of bullets are better still !

Blood. Damnation !

Bad. Derringer's self-cocking. Drop your hand, or I'll blow you into pi. So, you took me for a fool :—that's where you made a mistake. I took you for a thorough rascal, that's where I did *not* make a mistake. Now, to business.

Blood. [*Surlily.*] How much do you want ?

Bad. Fifty thousand dollars !

Blood. Be it so.

Bad. In gold, or Chemicals.

Blood. Very well. To-morrow——

Bad. No—to-night.

Blood. To-night !

Bad. Yes ; I wish to purchase a brown stone house on the avenue, early in the morning.

Blood. Come with me to my house in Madison Square.

Bad. No, thank you. I'll expect you here in an hour with the money.

Blood. [*Aside.*] He has me in his power—I must yield. [*Aloud.*] I will return, then, in an hour.

Bad. Let me light you out: Mind the bannister—don't break your precious neck, at least, not to-night. No, go in front, will you ? I prefer it.

Blood. What for ?

Bad. [*With pistol and candle.*] A fancy of mine—a want of confidence. A want of confidence, in fact, pervades the community. [*Exeunt.*]

[*Re-enter* Lucy.]

Lucy. I took a cross street, and ran rapidly home. Now I am alone ; the fumes of the charcoal will soon fill this small room. They say it is an easy death—but let me not hesitate— let me sleep the long sleep where there are no more tears, no more suffering. [*Exit into closet*, R. H.]

[*Re-enter* Badger.]

Bad. So ! that is settled. I hope he will be cautious and escape the garroters. James, my chiboque. [*Takes his pipe.*]

[*Re-enter* Mrs. Fairweather, R. H.]

Mrs. F. Poor Lucy ! I dared not look back upon her, as we parted forever. Despair hastened my steps. My poor children ! I have given you all I had, and now I hope my wretched life will serve you in your terrible need. Come, courage ; let me prevent the fresh air from entering. [*Takes bits of linen and stops window and door.*]

Bad. [*Snuffing.*] I smell charcoal—burning charcoal— where can it come from ?

Mrs. F. Now let me stop the door.

Bad. [*Smoking.*] It's very odd ; I've a queer feeling in my head ; let me lie down awhile. [*Lies on his bed.*]

[*Enter* **Lucy,** *with a brazier of charcoal, alight.*]

Mrs. F. That's done. [*Going towards closet, and meeting* **Lucy.**] Now the hour has come.

Lucy. The moment has arrived. [*Sets down the brazier.*]

Mrs. F. Lucy !

Lucy. Mother !

Mrs. F. My child, what is this ? For what purpose are you here ?

Lucy. And you, mother, why have you fastened those apertures so closely ? Like me, you wished to die !

Mrs. F. No, no, you shall not die ! my darling child—you are young—life is before you—hope—happiness.

Lucy. The future ! what is it ? The man I love will soon wed another. I have no future, and the present is a torture.

Mrs. F. Hush, my child, hush !

Lucy. Is it not better to die thus, than by either grief or hunger ?

Mrs. F. [*Falling in a chair.*] Already my senses fail me. Lucy, my child, live, live !

Lucy. [*Falls at her feet.*] No ; let us die together—thus, mother—as often I knelt to you as a child, let me pray for those we love.

Mrs. F. Oh, merciful Judge in Heaven, forgive us—forgive my child—and let—your anger fall—on me—alone——

Lucy. God bless my dear brother—and you, my dear Mark, may—you be—hap—— [*Murmurs the rest of the prayer.*]

Bad. It's very cold ! I feel quite sleepy. I must not go to sleep. [*Sings in a low voice.*] "Oh, down in ole Virginny."

Paul. [*Without knocking.*] Mother, open the door, why is the · door locked ? Mother, mother ! Open, mother, open ! [*Knocks violently.* **Mrs. Fairweather,** *arising, tries to reach the door, but cannot, and falls.* **Paul** *bursts open the door and enters with* **Livingstone** ; *they start back*—**Livingstone** *breaks the window, and* **Paul** *runs to his mother.*] Too late ! too late ! They have committed suicide !

Mark. They live still. Quick, bear them outside into the air. [*Carries* **Lucy** *out, while* **Paul** *assists his mother into the next room.*]

Bad. [*Starting up.*] How hot it is here—I cannot breathe. Have I drank too much ? Nonsense ! I could drink a dozen such bottles. Let me try my legs a bit—where's the door ? I can't see it—my head spins round—come, Badger, no nonsense now. God ! I'm suffocating ! Am I going to die, to die ! like

that old sea captain ? [*Tears off his cravat.*] Justice of
Heaven ! I am strangling. Help ! help ! Bloodgood will return
and find me helpless, then he will rob me of the receipt, as I
robbed the old sailor—I know him of old—he is capable of it,
but he shall not have it ! There, in its nook, if I have strength
to reach it—it is safe—safe. [*Drags himself along the floor,
lifts up a loose board, puts the receipt beneath it and falls
exhausted.*] There !

Paul. [*Entering* R. H. *room.*] I heard smothered cries for
help—they came from this floor. [*Exit.*]

[*Enter* **Bloodgood**, L. H. *room.*]

Blood. Here I am, Badger. [*Starts back, suffocated.*] What
a suffocating atmosphere ! where is he ? ha ! is he intoxicated ?

Paul. [*Entering* L. H. *room.*] Perhaps the cry came from
here—dead ?

Blood. Paul Fairweather !

Paul. Gideon Bloodgood !

Bad. [*Raising his head.*] What names were those ? Both
of them ! Together, here ! [*To* **Paul.**] Listen—while I yet
have breath to speak—listen ! Twenty years ago, that man
robbed your father of $100,000 !

Paul. Robbed !

Blood. Scoundrel !

Bad. I've got the proofs.

Paul. The proofs ?

Bad. I have 'em safe—you'll find 'em—th—ah ! [*Falls
backwards insensible ;* **Paul** *and* **Bloodgood** *stand aghast.*]

END OF ACT IV.

ACT V.

SCENE I.—*Brooklyn Heights, overlooking the city of New
York and its harbors. The stage is occupied by a neat garden,
on a natural terrace of the heights—on the* L. H., *a frame
cottage, prettily built—a table, with breakfast laid,* L. H., *at
which* **Mrs. Fairweather** *and* **Paul** *are seated.*

[*Enter* **Mrs. Puffy**, *from the cottage, with a teapot.*]

Mrs. P. There's the tea. Bless me, how hot it is to-day !
who would think that we were in the month of February ?
[*Sits.*]

Mrs. F. Your husband is late to breakfast.

Paul. Here he comes.

[*Enter* **Puffy**, *gaily.*]

Puffy. How is everybody? and above everybody, how is Miss Lucy this morning? [*Sits at table.*]

Mrs. F. Poor child! her recovery is slow—the fever has abated; but she is still very weak.

Paul. Her life is saved—for a whole month she hovered over the grave.

Puffy. But how is it we never see Mr. Livingstone? Our benefactor is like Santa Claus—he showers benefits and blessings on us all, yet never shows us his face.

Mrs. F. He brought us back to this, our old home—he obtained employment for Paul in the Navy Yard.

Puffy. He set me up again in my patent oven, and got me a Government contract for Navy biscuit.

Mrs. P. He is made of the finest flour that Heaven ever put into human baking; he'll die of over-bigness of the heart.

Mrs. F. That's a disease hereditary in your family.

Paul. [*Rising.*] I will tell you why Livingstone avoids our gratitude. Because my sister Lucy refused his love—because he has sold his hand to Alida Bloodgood—and he has given us the purchase money.

Puffy. And amongst those who have served us, don't let us forget poor Badger.

[*Enter* **Badger**, *behind.*]

Bad. They are talking of me.

Mrs. F. [*Rising.*] Forget him! forget the man who watched Lucy during her illness, with more than the tenderness of a brother! A woman never can forget any one who has been kind to her children.

Mrs. P. Them's my sentiments to a hair.

Bad. You shan't have cause to change them.

Paul. Badger!

Bad. Congratulate me. I have been appointed to the police. The commissioners wanted a special service to lay on to Wall Street. Roguery, it seems, has concentrated there, and we want to catch a big offender.

Mrs. P. They all go to Europe.

Puffy. That accounts for the drain of specie. [**Mr.** *and* **Mrs. Puffy** *take off the breakfast table.*]

Mrs. F. I will tell Lucy that her nurse has come. [*Exit into cottage.*]

Paul. Now, Badger, the news.

Bad. Bad, sir. To-night Mr. Livingstone is to be married to Alida Bloodgood.

Paul. What shall I do ? I dare not accuse Bloodgood of this robbery, unless you can produce the proofs—and perhaps the wretch has discovered and destroyed them.

Bad. I think not. When I recovered from the effects of the charcoal, the day after my suffocation, I started for my lodging —I found the house shut up, guarded by a servant of Bloodgood's —the banker had bought the place. But I had concealed the document too cunningly ; he has not found it.

Paul. But knowing this man to be a felon, whom we may be able at any hour to unmask, can we allow Livingstone to marry his daughter ?

[*Enter* **Livingstone.**]

Liv. Paul, I have come to bid you farewell, and to see Lucy for the last time.

[*Enter* **Lucy.**]

Lucy. For the last time, why so——   [**Paul** *and* **Badger** *run to assist her forward.*]

Liv. Lucy, dear Lucy !

Bad. Now take care—sit down.

Lucy. Ah, my good, kind nurse. [*She sits.*] You are always by my side.

Bad. Always ready with a dose of nasty medicine, ain't I— well now I've got another dose ready—do you see this noble kind heart, Lucy ; it looks through two honest blue eyes, into your face—well, tell me what you see there.

Lucy. Why do you ask me ? [*Troubled.*]

Bad. Don't turn your eyes away—the time has come when deception is a crime, Lucy—look in his face, and confess the infernal scheme by which Alida Bloodgood compelled you to renounce your love.

Liv. Alida !

Lucy. Has she betrayed me ?

Bad. No ! you betrayed yourself—one night in the ravings of your fever, when I held your hands in the paroxysm of your frenzy, I heard the cries that came from your poor wounded heart ; shall I repeat the scene ?

Lucy. [*Hiding her face in her hands.*] No, no !

Liv. Paul, is this true ? Have I been deceived ?

Paul. You have—Lucy confessed to me this infamous bargain, extorted from her by Alida Bloodgood, and to save you from ruin she sacrificed her love.

Liv. Lucy! dear Lucy, look up. It was for your sake alone that I accepted this hated union—to save you and yours from poverty—but whisper one word, tell me that ruin of fortune is better than ruin of the heart. [**Lucy** *falls upon his neck.*]

Bad. Hail Columbia! I know a grand party at Madison Square that will cave in to-night—hi !---I shall be there to congratulate that sweet girl.

[*Enter* **Dan.**]

Dan. Mother! mother! where's my hat, quick, there's a fire in New York. [*He runs into the house and re-enters with a telescope ; looks off towards the city.*]

Bad. Yes, and there is a fire here too, but one we don't want put out.

Paul. Now, Mark, I can confess to you that documents exist—proofs of felony against Bloodgood, which may at any moment consign him to the State prison, and transfer to our family his ill-gotten wealth.

Liv. Proofs of felony?

Dan. The fire is in Chatham Street.

Paul. Twenty years ago he robbed my father of $100,000.

Bad. And I was his accomplice in the act ; we shared the plunder between us.

Dan. No, it isn't in Chatham Street—I see it plainly—it is in Cross Street, Five Points.

Bad. [*Starting.*] Cross Street—where, where? [*Runs up.*]

Liv. But if these proofs--these documents exist, where are they?

Dan. It is the tenement house two doors from the corner.

Bad. Damnation! it is our old lodging! you ask where are these proofs, these documents? they are yonder, in that burning house—fired by Bloodgood to destroy the papers he could not find—curses on him!

[*Enter* **Mrs. Puffy,** *with* **Dan's** *hat.*]

Mrs. P. Here's your hat, Dan.

Bad. Quick! Dan, my son—for our lives! Dan! the fortunes of Lucy, and Paul, and the old woman, are all in that burning house. [**Dan** *begins to thrust his trousers into his boots. Enter* **Mrs. Fairweather** *and* **Puffy.**] I mean to save it or perish in the flames.

Dan. Count me in. [*They run out.*]

[*Tableau.*]

SCENE II.—*Stage dark. The exterior of the tenement house, No. 19½ Cross Street, Five Points—the shutters of all the windows are closed. A light is seen through the round holes in the shutters of the upper windows—presently a flame rises—it is extinguished—then revives. The light seen to descend as the bearer of it passes down the staircase, the door opens cautiously —* **Bloodgood,** *disguised, appears—he looks round—closes the door again—locks it.*

Blood. In a few hours, this accursed house will be in ruins. The receipt is concealed there—and it will be consumed in the flames. [*The glow of fire is seen to spread from room to room.*] Now, Badger—do your worst—I am safe ! [*Exit.*]

[*The house is gradually enveloped in fire, a cry outside is heard, "Fi-er!" "Fi-er!" It is taken up by other voices more distant. The tocsin sounds—other churches take up the alarm—bells of engines are heard. Enter a crowd of persons. Enter* **Badger,** *without coat or hat—he tries the door—finds it fast ; seizes a bar of iron and dashes in the ground floor window, the interior is seen in flames. Enter* **Dan.***

Dan. [*Seeing* **Badger** *climbing into the window.*] Stop! stop!

[**Badger** *leaps in and disappears. Shouts from the mob ;* **Dan** *leaps in—another shout,* **Dan** *leaps out again black and burned, staggers forward and seems overcome by the heat and smoke. The shutters of the garret fall and discover* **Badger** *in the upper floor. Another cry from the crowd, a loud crash is heard,* **Badger** *disappears as if falling with the inside of the building. The shutters of the windows fall away, and the inside of the house is seen, gutted by the fire ; a cry of horror is uttered by the mob.* **Badger** *drags himself from the ruins, and falls across the sill of the lower window.* **Dan** *and two of the mob run to help him forward but recoil before the heat ; at length they succeed in rescuing his body, which lies* C. **Livingstone, Paul,** *and* **Puffy,** *rush on.* **Dan** *kneels over* **Badger** *and extinguishes the fire which clings to parts of his clothes.*]

SCENE III.—*The drawing-room in* **Bloodgood's** *mansion, in Madison Square—illuminated. Music within.*

[*Enter* **Bloodgood.**]

Blood. The evidence of my crime is destroyed no power— on earth can reveal the past. [*Enter* **Alida,** *dressed as a* *bride.*] My dearest child, to-night you will leave this roof ; but from this home in your father's heart none can displace you.

Alida. Oh, dear papa, do take care of my flounces—you men paw one about as if a dress was put on only to be rumpled.

Blood. The rooms below are full of company. Has Livingstone arrived ?

Alida. I did not inquire. The Duke is there, looking the picture of misery, while all my female friends pretend to congratulate me—but I know they are dying with envy and spite.

Blood. And do these feelings constitute the happiest day of your life ? Alida, have you no heart ?

Alida. Yes, father, I have a heart—but it is like yours. It is an iron safe in which are kept the secrets of the past.

[*Enter* **Edwards.**]

Edw. The clergyman is robed, sir, and ready to perform the ceremony.

Blood. Let the bridesmaids attend Miss Bloodgood. [*The curtains are raised, and the* **Bridesmaids** *enter.* **Bloodgood** *goes up and off, and immediately returns with the bridal party.*] Welcome, my kind friends. [**Alida** *speaks aside with the* **Duke.**] Your presence fills me with pride and joy—but where is the bridegroom ? has no one seen my son-in-law ?

Edw. [*Announcing.*] Mr. Mark Livingstone.

[*Enter* **Livingstone.**]

Blood. Ah ! at last. What a strange costume for a bridegroom.

Alida. [*Turns, and views* **Livingstone.**] Had I not good reasons to be assured of your sincerity, Mr. Livingstone, your appearance would lead me to believe that you look upon this marriage as a jest, or a masquerade.

Liv. As you say, Miss Bloodgood, it is a masquerade—but it is one where more than one mask must fall.

Blood. [*Aside.*] What does he mean ?

Alida. You speak in a tone of menace. May——

Blood. Perhaps I had better see Mr. Livingstone alone—he may be under some misapprehension.

Liv. I am under none, sir—although you may be ; and what I have to say and do, demands no concealment. I come here to decline the hand of your daughter. [*Movement amongst the crowd.*]

Blood. You must explain this public insult.

4

Liv. I am here to do so, but I do not owe this explanation to you ; I owe it to myself, and those friends I see here, whose presence under your roof is a tribute to the name I bear. My friends, I found myself in this man's debt ; he held in pledge all I possessed—all but my name ; that name he wanted to shelter the infamy in which his own was covered ; I was vile enough to sell it.

Blood. Go on, sir ; go on.

Liv. With your leave, I will.

Alida. These matters you were fully acquainted with, I presume, when you sought my hand.

Liv. But I was not acquainted with the contents of these letters—written by you, to the Duke of Calcavella.

Blood. Dare you insinuate that they contain evidence derogatory to the honor of my child ?

Liv. No, sir ; but I think Miss Bloodgood will agree with me, that the sentiments expressed in these letters entitle her to the hand of the Duke, rather than to mine. [*He hands the letters to* **Alida.**]

Alida. Let him go, father.

Liv. Not yet. You forget that my friends here are assembled to witness a marriage, and all we require is a bride.

Blood. Yes ; a bride who can pay your debts.

[*Enter* **Paul, Lucy,** *and* **Mrs. Fairweather.**]

Paul. No, sir ; a bride who can place the hand of a pure and loving maiden in that of a good and honest man.

Blood. How dare you intrude in this house ?

Paul. Because it is mine ; because your whole fortune will scarcely serve to pay the debt you owe the widow and the children of Adam Fairweather.

Blood. Is my house to be invaded by beggars like these ! Edwards, send for the police. Is there no law in New York for ruffians ?

[*Enter* **Badger,** *in the uniform of an officer of police.*]

Bad. Yes, plenty—and here's the police.

Blood. Badger !

Bad. What's left of him.

Blood. [*Wildly.*] Is this a conspiracy to ruin me ?

Bad. That's it. We began it twenty years ago ; we've been hatching it ever since ; we let you build up a fortune ; we tempted you to become an incendiary ; we led you on from misdemeanor to felony—and that's what I want you for.

Blood. What do you mean ?

Bad. My meaning is set forth very clearly in an affidavit, on which the Recorder, at this very late hour for business, issued this warrant for your arrest.

[*Enter* **Two Policemen.** **Alida** *falls in a chair.*]

Blood. Incendiary ! Dare you charge a man of my standing in this city, with such a crime, without any cause ?

Bad. Cause ! you wanted to burn up this receipt, which I was just in time to rescue from the flames !

Blood. [*Drawing a knife.*] Fiend ! you escaped the flames here—now go to those hereafter !

Bad. Hollo ! [*Disarms* **Bloodgood,** *and slips a pair of handcuffs on him.*] Gideon—my dear Gideon—don't lose your temper. [*Throws him back, manacled, on the sofa.*]

Paul. Miss Bloodgood, let me lead you from this room.

Alida. [*Rises, and crosses to her father.*] Father !

Blood. Alida, my child.

Alida. Is this true ? [*A pause.*] It is—I read it in your quailing eye—on your paling lips. And it was for this that you raised me to the envied position of a rich man's heiress—for this you roused my pride—for this you decked me in jewels—to be the felon's daughter. Farewell.

Blood. Alida—my child—my child—it was for you alone I sinned—do not leave me.

Alida. What should I do in this city ? can I earn my bread ? what am I fit for—with your tainted name and my own sad heart ? [*Throws down her bride's coronet.*] I am fit for the same fate as yours—infamy. [*Exit.*]

Bad. Duke, you had better see that lady out. [*Exit* **Duke.**] Gideon, my dear, allow me to introduce you to two friends of mine, who are anxious to make your acquaintance.

Blood. Take me away ; I have lost my child—my Alida ; take me away ; hide me from all the world.

Paul. Stay ! Mr. Bloodgood, in the midst of your crime there was one virtue : you loved your child ; even now your heart deplores her ruin—not your own. Badger, give me that receipt. [*Takes the receipt from* **Badger.**] Do you acknowledge this paper to be genuine ?

Blood. I do.

Paul. [*Tears it.*] I have no charge against you. Let him be released. Restore to me my fortune, and take the rest ; go, follow your child ; save her from ruin, and live a better life.

Blood. I cannot answer you as I would. [*Turns aside in* *tears, and goes out with* **Policemen** *and* **Badger,** *who releases* **Bloodgood.**]

Liv. That was nobly done, Paul. Now, my friends, since all is prepared for my marriage let the ceremony proceed.

Mrs. F. But where is Mrs. Puffy.

Bad. Here they are, outside, but they won't come in.

Paul. Why not ?

Bad. They are afraid of walking on the carpets.

Liv. Bring them in.

Bad. That's soon done. [*Exit.*]

Mrs. F. Poor, good, kind people—the first to share our sorrow, the last to claim a part in our joy.

[*Enter* **Badger** *and* **Dan**—**Puffy** *and one* **Policeman**—**Mrs. Puffy** *and the other* **Policeman.**]

Bad. They wouldn't come—I was obliged to take 'em in custody.

Dan. Oh ! mother, where's this ?

Mrs. P. I'm walkin' on a feather bed.

Puffy. He wouldn't let me wipe my shoes.

Liv. Come in—these carpets have never been trodden by more honest feet, these mirrors have never reflected kinder faces—come in—breathe the air here—you will purify it.

Mrs. P. Oh, Dan, what grand folks—ain't they ?

Dan. Canvas backs every one on 'em.

Liv. And now, Lucy, I claim your hand. [*Music inside.*] All is ready for the ceremony.

Bad. You have seen the dark side of life—you can appreciate your fortune, for you have learned the value of wealth.

Mrs. F. No, we have learned the value of poverty. [*Gives her hand to* **Puffy.**] It opens the heart.

Paul. [*To the public.*] Is this true ? Have the sufferings we have depicted in this mimic scene, touched your hearts, and caused a tear of sympathy to fill your eyes ? If so, extend to us your hands.

Mrs. F. No, not to us—but when you leave this place, as you return to your homes, should you see some poor creatures, extend your hands to them, and the blessings that will follow you on your way will be the most grateful tribute you can pay to the poor of the

STREETS OF NEW YORK.

The American Amateur Drama.

A collection of new copyrighted plays, suitable for amateur and professional performances. The acting is not especially difficult, and the scenery can be easily managed. While full of action, these plays are not boisterous, but are refined and elevated in tone. They are bright, interesting and contain not a dull line. Before deciding on a drama for amateur performance, read these plays.

Aroused at Last. Comedy in one act, by Mary Kyle Dallas. Four male, four female characters. Plays about forty minutes. One interior parlor scene. Costumes of to-day; scene, New York City. A play full of brisk but refined action, lively dialogue, and the comedy possibilities are unlimited. Mr. and Mrs. Pondicherry are a successful business man and his fond wife. Mr. and Mrs. Vandernoodle, a young old Knickerbocker and his bride. Miss and Mr. Wiggins, a spinster from Toadfish Point and her brother, Celeste, a breezy French maid and a young man waiter complete a fine cast of characters. Price, 15 cents.

Bloomer Girls, or, Courtship in the Twentieth Century. Satirical comedy in one act, by John A. Fraser, Jr., author "Noble Outcast," "Modern Ananias," "A Cheerful Liar," etc. One male, three female characters. One garden scene, which may be changed to an interior if desired. Plays two hours. Two young women in handsome bloomer costumes, one elderly lady in dark dress and a very effiminately attired young man compose the cast of characters. The dialogue is written in Mr. Fraser's best style—bright and refined, while at the same time it hits the fad hard. Price, 15 cents.

Bold Stratagem. Comedy in three acts, by Marsden Brown. Four male, three female characters; costumes modern; one exterior, two interior scenes. Plays forty-five minutes. This sparkling comedy is bright and witty, yet pure in tone, having no elaborate costumes or difficult scenery. Amateurs will find it just what they want. Every character good. Every situation telling. Price, 15 cents.

Burglars. Comedy in one act, by Robert Julian, author of "Will You Marry Me?" Two male, two female characters. A parlor scene. Plays fifteen minutes. Costumes are suitable for one lady and one gentleman in the fashion of to-day, for a housemaid's pretty dress and a young dandy darkey. The cast includes Mrs. Greene, afraid of burglars; her husband, brave when there is no danger; Kitty, afraid of no one, and Toby, a darkey, who is hired to catch burglars. The situations are new, and will keep the audience roaring from the entrance of Toby to the end. Price, 15 cents.

Cheerful Liar. Farcical comedy in three acts, by John A. Fraser, Jr., author of "Modern Ananias," "Noble Outcast," "Merry Cobbler," etc. Five male, three female characters. Plays three hours. Three interior scenes, all easily arranged. Costumes of the day. A shrieking farcical comedy, full of "go" and new situations. Unlike most light pieces, this one has a most capital plot, full of entanglements. It is a comedy in which any number of specialties may be introduced, although it was played on the professional stage a long season without any. Flora, Randolph, Guy, Hussel and Mrs. Sweetlove may all sing and dance with advantage. Judge Hussel is a great character part. The audacity as well as cheerfulness with which he prevaricates invariably "brings down the house." In the last act where Flora dons a boy's costume and the Judge is dressed to captivate, the stage presents one of the strongest comedy scenes that has ever been suggested. The book of the play gives the very full stage directions for crosses, entrances, exits, etc., for which Mr. Fraser's plays are noted. While prepared for amateurs in details, professional companies find this play a good one for the box office as well as an artistic favorite. Price, 25 cents.

Delicate Question. Comedy drama in four acts, by John A. Fraser, Jr., author of "Modern Ananias," "Noble Outcast," etc. Nine male, three female characters. One exterior, two interior scenes. Modern costumes. Plays two hours. If a play presenting an accurate picture of life in the rura. districts is required, in which every character has been faithfully studied from life, nothing better for the use of amateurs than "A Delicate Question" can be recommended. The story is utterly unlike that of any other play, and deals with the saloon, which it handles without gloves and at the same time without a single line of sermonizing. What "Ten Nights in a Barroom" was to the public of a past generation, "A Delicate Question" is destined to be to the present, although it is far from being exactly what is known as a "temperance play." The plot is intensely interesting, the pathetic scenes full of beauty, because they are mental photographs from nature, and the comedy is simply uproariously funny. The parts, very equally balanced. The scenic effects are quite simple, and by a little ingenuity the entire piece may be played in a kitchen scene. The climaxes are all as novel as they are effective and the dialogue is as natural as if the characters were all real people. Price, 25 cents.

Food for Powder. Vaudeville in two acts, by R. Andre, author of "A Handsome Cap," "Minette's Birthday," etc. Three male, two female characters. One interior scene. Plays forty minutes. Costumes, French, of the time of Napoleon I. This dainty and refined play is full of pretty songs set to familiar airs, and specialty dances may be introduced. For professional or amateur vaudeville evenings, this will be found just the thing for the short drama which should always form one of the features. Price, 15 cents.

Handsome Cap. Comic operetta in one act, by R. Andre, author of "Food for Powder," "Minette's Birthday," etc. Three male, two female characters. One cottage interior scene. Costumes, of time of George II.. Plays forty minutes. The songs are all written to be sung to popular and well-known airs; dances may be introduced without limit, although there is a real plot and story carried to a happy termination. Like. other plays by this writer, "A Handsome Cap" is peculiarly suited to amateur and professional vaudeville evenings. Price, 15 cents.

Maud Muller. Operetta in three acts, by Effie W. Merriman, author "Socials," "Pair of Artists," etc. Three male, two female characters. Ludicrous costumes and some property effects which may be easily arranged but are very amusing. One interior, one exterior scene. Plays two hours. The piece is arranged for a chorus to do a good deal of work, but a distinct reader will be found effective. The book of the play gives the most minute directions for its production as to action and properties. The horse upon which the judge rides in the hay-field scene is represented by two men covered by a fur robe. The antics of this horse may be made as funny as the imagination of the director may suggest. The judge should be a spare man made up to look pompous. Church societies, as well as amateur clubs. will find this a money-making entertainment. Price, 25 cents.

Merry Cobbler. Comedy drama in four acts, by John A. Fraser, Jr., author "Bloomer Girls," "Showman's Ward." "Modern Ananias," etc. Six male, five female characters. Two interior, two exterior scenes. Modern costumes. Plays two hours. This romantic story of a German emigrant boy who falls in love with, and finally marries, a dashing Southern belle, is one of the cleanest and daintiest in the whole repertoire of the minor stage. The Merry Cobbler is one of the type the late J. K Emmet so loved to portray. Had the piece been originally written for the use of amateurs it could not have been happier in its results, its natural and mirth-provoking comedy combined with a strong undercurrent of heart interest, rendering it a vehicle with which even inexperienced actors are sure to be seen at their best. The scenic effects are of the simplest description and the climaxes, while possessing the requisite amount of "thrill" are very easy to handle. The author has prepared elaborate instructions for its production by amateur players. Price, 25 cents.

Minette's Birthday. Vaudeville in one act, by R. Andre, author of "A Handsome Cap," "Food for Powder," etc. Two male, three female characters. Plays forty-five minutes. One interior cottage scene. Costumes, in fancy French peasant fashion. This is another one of this author's plays arranged for the popular amateur and professional vaudeville evenings. It i. full of merry songs and dances, refined, spirited and very amusing always. Price, 15 cents.

Modern Ananias. Comedy in three acts, by John A. Fraser, Jr., author " Noble Outcast," " Showman's Ward," etc. Four male, four female characters. Two interior, one exterior scenes. Modern society costumes. Plays three hours. This is a screaming farcical comedy, which depends upon the wit and humor of its lines no less than upon the drollery and absurdity of its situations for the shrieks of laughter it invariably provokes. Unlike most farcical comedies. " A Modern Ananias" has an ingeniously complicated plot, which maintains a keen dramatic interest until the fall of the last curtain. The scenery, if necessary, may be reduced to a garden scene and an interior. The climaxes are all hilariously funny, and each of the three acts is punctured with laughs from beginning to end. Amateurs will find nothing more satisfactory in the whole range of the comic drama than this up-to-date comedy-farce. The fullest stage directions accompany the book, including all the "crosses" and positions, pictures, etc. Price, 25 cents.

Noble Outcast. Drama in four acts, by John A. Fraser, Jr., author " Modern Ananias,"" Merry Cobbler,"" Cheerful Liar,"etc. Four male, three female characters. Plays three hours. Costumes, modern, except Jerry's, when he appears as a tramp and again as an exaggerated "swell." This play has proven one of the most popular ever produced on the professional stage, but the author for the first time now allows it to be printed from the original manuscript. All the entrances, exits and positions will be found in the book of the play. It is safe to say that in the whole range of the drama there is no character to be found with such power to compel alternate laughter and tears as is shown by "Jerry, the tramp." The dramatic interest is always intense. Price, 25 cents.

Pair Of Artists. Comedy in three acts, by Effie W. Merriman, author of " Maud Muller,"" Socials,"etc. Four male, three female characters. Plays one and three-quarters hours. Three interior scenes, all easily arranged. Mrs. Scott wears bloomers and a man's hat; Mr.Scott, blue overalls and a checked gingham apron; Gertie, a long-sleeved apron and hair braided down her back; the others, conventional dress of to-day. Each character has a prominent part. There is no villain or heavy people; all goes with a vim, and has been presented to the most critical audiences with entire success. Price, 15 cents.

Purse, The. Comedy in two acts; dramatized by Theodore Harris, from Balzac's "La Bourse." Seven male, two female characters. Plays one hour and fifty minutes. Interior scenes. costumes of the time of Napoleon I. The exquisite language and sentiment of this noted French writer has been admirably translated by Mr. Harris. For a student of dramatic literature, this part is recommended. The dialogue is as dainty and charming as a piece of French porcelain. Price, 15 cents.

Showman's Ward. Comedy in three acts, by John A. Fraser, Jr., author of "Noble Outcast," "Delicate Question," "Merry Cobbler," etc. Eight male, five female characters. Three doubles may be made. Costumes of to-day. Plays two and one-half hours, This comedy has been very successfully performed under another title on the professional stage. It is, however, well adapted for the use of amateurs on account of the absence of scenic effects, the play being capable of performance in a parlor with different furniture for each act. The more singing and dancing introduced, the better for the performance. There is a dress rehearsal scene and a girls' school scene, which are always uproariously funny. The number of girls taking part in the school scene may be unlimited, thus making the play an admirable one for a club or society. The role of the showman's ward is a soubrette one, and it can easily be made a star part by a clever young woman if this is desired. Still, all the characters are so distinctly drawn that each is important and leading. Mr. Fraser has, as usual, given full directions for the stage production of this comedy in the book of the play. Price, 25 cents.

Twixt Love and Money. Comedy drama in four acts, by John A. Fraser, Jr., author "Modern Ananias," "Merry Cobbler," "Noble Outcast," etc. Eight male, three female characters. Plays two and one-half hours. Three interior scenes. Costumes of the day. This charming domestic comedy drama of the present day bids fair to rival, both with professionals and amateurs, the success of "Hazel Kirke." The scene is laid in a little village on the coast of Maine, and the action is replete with dramatic situations which "play themselves." The story is intensely interesting and, in these days of Frenchy adaptations and "problem" plays, delightfully pure; while the moral—that love brings more happiness than does money—is plainly pointed without a single line of preaching. No such romantic interest has been built up around a simple, country heroine since the production of "Hazel Kirke" and "May Blossom" years ago. The play is in four acts, and as the scenery is easy to manage it is particularly well adapted for the use of amateurs. This play was originally written for professionals, but has been carefully revised for amateurs by Mr. Fraser, and the book contains full directions for all stage business. The dramatic interest is intense, each act being given a strong climax in situation and dialogue. Price, 25 cents.

Will You Marry Me? Farce in one act, by Robert Julian, author of "Burglars." Two male, two female characters. Plays twenty minutes. Costumes of to-day for eccentric old gentleman, one maiden elderly lady, one young man and one young woman. One interior parlor scene. The plot is full of intensely amusing matrimonial complications, with a happy ending. The fun is about evenly divided among the four strong parts. Some clever acting is desired where the dialogue is repeated under contrasting circumstances, by different persons. Price, 15 cents.

The World Acting Drama.

Price, 15 Cents.

This collection of plays contains only such as are world-wide in popularity. Some are suitable for the amateur stage, some for the professional stage, some for both. The farces are sparkling, the comedies witty, the dramas and trage. dies thrilling, but nothing dull, impure or suggestive is admitted. The plays are printed from large clear type, on good paper, and are undoubtedly superior to all other editions in the market.

Betsy Baker. Farce in one act, by J. Madison Morton, author of "Box and Cox," "Slasher and Crasher," etc. Two male, two female characters. Parlor scene. Plays forty-five minutes. Costumes, simple ones of to-day. Wherever this farce is presented it is received with the greatest enthusiasm They are all star parts.

Box and Cox. Romance in real life, in one act, by J. Madison Morton, author of "Poor Pillicoddy," "Betsy Baker," etc. Two male, one female characters. Plays thirty-five minutes. Plain every-day costumes. One plainly furnished room. There is no other farce that has been given as often and as successfully as "Box and Cox." It always keeps an audience in a continual roar of laughter.

By Special Desire. Drawing-room monologue for a lady in one interior scene. Usually plays fifteen minutes. The usual evening or afternoon dress can be worn. This is best given by one possessing a simple unaffected style.

Cool as a Cucumber. Farce in one act, by W. Blanchard Jerrold. Three male, two female characters. Plays fifty minutes. Parlor scene. Costumes of to-day. Star part for a dashing young comedian, with other characters well-drawn. The play is rich in opportunities and dramatic situations.

Cricket on the Hearth, or, A Fairy Tale of Home. Drama in three acts, dramatized by Albert Smith from Charles Dickens' story of the same name. Seven male, eight female characters, besides fairies and neighbors. Two interior scenes. Costumes of fifty years ago. Plays two hours. Invariably witnessed with enthusiasm.

Daughter-in-Law. Comedietta in one act, by Mary Seymour. Four female characters. Plays thirty minutes. Interior scene. Modern costumes. This is a first-class play for a curtain-raiser or to give in connection with a broader farcical comedy. It is very refined, but spirited.

Fast Friends. Comedietta in one act, by R. Henry, author of "A Narrow Escape," etc. Two female characters. Modern costumes. Plays twenty minutes. Interior scene. A very amusing little play, which is always well received, where. ever given. Full of action and bright dialogue.

Gringoire. Pathetic play in one act, translated from the French of De Banville by Arthur Shirley. Four male, two female characters. Interior scene. Louis XI. costumes. Plays forty minutes. Nat. Goodwin has made this a most successful play in his repertoire, but it is also easily given by amateurs.

Hamlet. Tragedy, by William Shakespeare, arranged in five acts by Mr. Wilson Barrett. Nineteen male, three female characters. Plays two hours. The action of this edition is carefully indicated, and the large clear type makes it a specially good one for students and public readers.

Hidden Hand. Drama in five acts, by Robert Jones, arranged from Mrs. E. D. E. N. Southworth's celebrated novel. Fifteen male, seven female characters. Costumes modern. Plays two and one-half hours. Four interior, two exterior scenes. A thrilling drama, with strong comedy scenes as well. One excellent negro part.

Ici on Parle Francais. Farce in one act, by Thomas J. Williams, author of "Larkin's Love Letters," etc. Three male, four female characters. One interior scene. One military and costumes of to-day. Plays forty minutes. This is one of the best of farces. Every character is good and all goes with a rush.

Kathleen Mavourneen, or St. Patrick's Eve. Domestic Irish drama in four acts. Twelve male, four female characters. Three interior, two exterior scenes. Irish costumes. Plays two and one-quarter hours. The most popular Irish play ever written. Contains an unusual variety of characters and incidents, and it always takes well with audiences.

Lend Me Five Shillings. Farce in one act, by J. Madison Morton, author of "Betsy Baker," etc. Five male, two female characters. Interior scene. Evening costumes. Plays forty minutes. Joseph Jefferson and Nat. Goodwin consider Mr. Golightly one of their best parts. The play is uproariously funny.

Loan of a Lover. Vaudeville in one act, by J. R. Planche. Four male, two female characters. One military costume for gentleman, one outdoor dress for a lady, and the others wear picturesque peasants' dress. Garden scene. Plays fifty minutes. This play affords fine opportunities to introduce songs and dances.

Mistletoe Bough. Pantomime entertainment in five scenes, arranged from the well-known ballad by Henry R. Bishop. Two male, four female characters, Fifty ladies and gentlemen and as many children often take part, although a less number present it excellently. Plays two hours. Play gives full directions for production and costumes,

Mrs. Willis' Will. Comedy drama in one act, adapted from the French of Emile Souvestre. Five female characters. Interior scene. Modern costumes. Plays forty minutes. A country jig danced under protest by two of the ladies creates much fun. All the characters, as well as the moral, are good.

Obstinate Family. Farce in one act, arranged from the German. Three male, three female characters. Interior scene. Costumes of to-day. Plays forty minutes. Augustin Daly's company presented this play as "A Woman's Won't." It is also called "Thank Goodness, the Table is Spread." The play is delightfully entertaing and always successful.

Our Boys. Comedy in three acts, by Henry J. Byron. Six male, four female characters. Modern costumes. Three interior scenes. Plays two hours. By many, this is considered the most successful play ever written. Fine for professionals, but also easily produced by amateurs, as scenery is easily arranged.

Petticoat Perfidy. Comedietta in one act, by Sir Charles L. Young, author of "Jim the Penman," "Drifted Apart," etc. Threefe male characters. An interior scene. Modern costumes. Plays forty minutes. Bright little society comedy, full of wit and very amusing situations.

Pygmalion and Galatea. Mythological comedy in three acts, by W. S. Gilbert, author of all the librettos of Gilbert and Sullivan's operas. Five male, four female characters. Grecian costumes. Studio scene. Plays one hour and three-quarters. Acknowledged one of the most charming comedies.

Sunset. Comedy in one act, by Jerome K. Jerome. Three male, three female characters. Drawing-room scene. Modern costumes. Plays fifty minutes. This play has been successful on both the English and American stage. It is suitable also for amateurs. Requires some acting with reserve force in both comedy and pathos.

Sweethearts. Comedy in two acts, by W. S. Gilbert, author of "Pygmalion and Galatea," etc. Two male, two female characters. One garden scene. Modern costumes. Plays one hour. A delightful modern comedy, which ends happily after some misunderstandings. It is written in Gilbert's best style, which is always bright.

Ten Years Hence. Comedy in two acts, by Mary Seymour, author of "A Daughter-in-Law," etc. Five female characters. One interior, one exterior scenes. Plays one hour. Modern costumes. Marie is an excellent child's part. For a small play this comedy has a strong plot, which holds every audience.

To Oblige Benson. Comedietta in one act, by Tom Taylor, author of "Retribution," "Fool's Revenge," etc. Three male, two female characters. Interior scene. Modern costumes. Plays fifty minutes. An exceedingly lively play with a very amusing plot and plenty of action. The scene is easily arranged for a parlor.

Who's to Win Him. Comedietta in one act, by Thomas J. Williams, author of "Ici on Parle Francais," "Turn Him Out," etc. Three male, five female characters. Garden scene. Modern costumes. Plays fifty minutes. A very lively play, and admirably adapted for amateurs.